I0669043

BEYOND THE BATTLEFIELD:

A MESSAGE FROM THE FALLEN

Ken Dauth

Beyond the Battlefield: A Message from the Fallen
Copyright © 2012 by Ken Dauth

All rights reserved. No part of this book may be reproduced or
transmitted in any form or by any means without written permission
of the author and publisher.

This is a work of fiction. Any resemblance to actual persons, living or
dead, is purely coincidental.

ISBN: 978-0-9850066-0-0

Library of Congress Control Number: 2012932359

Cover design by All Things That Matter Press

Published in 2012 by All Things That Matter Press

To Sandy, my wife, my best friend, my foundation and my North Star

------

To Lori who yelled at me in the summer of 2008

Thanks Dad

ONE

If I could just hold my place—I found it; it is mine. There is nothing out there for me.

The morning finally came upon them even though they were not really prepared for daylight. A small truck rattled and rocked across the field, engine revving, making its way over crevices and around large, upturned rocks. Every eye watched it, hoping the driver would notice them on his way to the road.

"What's he doing?" Roy Johnson whispered.

"Trying to get to the road," Joe Williams responded.

Johnson was a big man, well over six feet tall. His blond hair stuck out from under his helmet, almost covering his soft brown eyes. Dirt smudges lurked in the stubble of his beard.

"How much further does he have to go?" Johnson asked. Williams pointed to a post by the road a few hundred yards in front of the truck.

Williams had his helmet pushed back, revealing a wide forehead covered with long, dried lines of sweat tracing toward his blue eyes. His constant blinking, usually a distraction, was necessary as he tried to focus in these predawn moments.

The truck slowed, just barely inching through the rough field. Before coming to a complete stop, the passenger door opened. A soldier stepped out—hunched over, head down, his back to Johnson and Williams moving along, using the truck as protection. He waved to the driver to turn left, avoiding a large hole and whatever other obstacles might be there.

The truck stopped suddenly, springs groaning. The soldier knelt down looking at a shadow in a shadow. He picked up an arm, holding it by the wrist.

Checking for a pulse

The soldier quickly reached into his pocket and pulled out something too tiny to be seen. Hitting it against his leg, it made a small but audible "crack" as it split open.

Johnson and Williams ducked their heads when they heard the sound, still surreptitiously surveying the field. The soldier stuck the arm with the object and then waved for the driver to back up. He pulled, lifting the slumped body over his shoulder before moving quickly toward the waiting truck. "We have to get that medic's attention!" Williams said. He bobbed his head up, then quickly dropped back down. A side door on the truck opened. Two pairs of bandaged arms pulled the body from the struggling medic and hauled it, arms flapping and feet— one sock-covered and the other shoe-covered—inside. The door shut, the engine revved and the truck lurched forward again, bouncing as it moved slowly toward the post marking the road.

Smoke drifted in and off the field; burning smells thickened the air. This day was as the day before: different hole, different field, same horizon. Johnson sometimes prayed out loud for smoke. Who needed horizons when there was no place to go?

He slid awkwardly along the ground, causing more noise than was safe. Every time he moved forward, a dragging scrapping sound seemed to echo from his shoes. Williams followed a short way behind, his dirty, blistered hands pulling him through the sand, trying to keep his head down while looking around.

Sergeant Gabriel Gordon watched from the corner of a hole under a broken wall, where he'd been placed during the night in an attempt to give him as much protection as could be found in the dark. Trails of blood marked where he'd been dragged.

Johnson rolled into a part of the field that was much lower and turned to Williams, signaling him to advance. Skidding along the ground as quickly as possible, Williams rolled in beside him with a grunt. They pushed their helmets down to their eyebrows and slowly poked their heads up to watch the truck rocking and squealing its way across the field, still at least a hundred yards away from the post.

Across the field a lone figure stood silhouetted in the smoke. The dim light and swirling smoke made it impossible to tell which way he was looking. Gordon tried to get Johnson's attention. A loud sound came from the truck as its front wheel hit in a hole; the lone figure crouched low until the truck managed to continue on its way.

Someone else appeared in the smoke, crouching down next to the first, waiting a moment before moving away from where the truck was headed, occasionally standing upright and turning to look back. Johnson was still not looking in Gordon's direction.

Williams wrote something on a piece of paper he pulled from his shirt pocket and handed it to Johnson. He then tapped Johnson on the shoulder, using his head to indicate he was going back where they came from.

Gordon looked at the two dark figures across the field, now bent so low to the ground he guessed they were moving on all fours. A small, rounded shadow popped up in the area they were headed. *Was it a helmet?*

Williams was back, scratching around in the dirt at the bottom of the hole looking for something and occasionally checking on Johnson. This really is not the time to be searching in the dark, Gordon thought. He tried to get Williams' attention, knowing anything too loud would attract an unwanted response from the other side of the field. Williams didn't respond; he just kept poking in the dirt.

The round figure popped up once again in the smoke and started to move, followed closely by two others, all still crawling in the opposite direction of the truck's journey.

Williams moved a large piece of wood; it hit the ground with a thump, pushing a cloud of dust ten feet into the air. Those in the shadows heard it, turned, and looked. Another round object appeared in the smoke, another helmet... that made four against three; with Gordon wounded, four against two.

Under the piece of wood that Williams had moved was a munitions box. He opened it, taking out a band of bullets that he put over his shoulder. After glancing at Gordon, he turned his head toward the far side of the field and flattened out, realizing he'd made too much noise. Crawling on his belly, he started making his way back to Johnson, the munitions belt scraping along the ground beside him.

An arm raised in shadows across the field, pointing to where Williams was moving. A puff of smoke appeared next to Williams' left arm, followed by the sharp sound of the round. Williams lay flat.

Johnson turned, took his rifle and pointed it in the direction of the shadows. One of the shadows fell as his first shot struck home. The other three returned fire. Johnson ducked into the hole, holding on to his helmet, as bullets hit the dirt just above his head.

The truck stopped briefly and then resumed its trek across the field. It was about forty feet from the post and accelerating, rocking back and forth from the strain of too much speed on a too old machine. Johnson shot a look its way before pulling his gun close and squeezing off another round, which dropped one more shadow and prompted heavier return fire.

Williams raised his hand to Johnson, then grabbed the munitions belt and tried to throw it. It fell short, landing a good away from Johnson.

The two remaining shadows on the other side of the field split, one running right and the other running left. Johnson took a chance and made a dash for the belt. After grabbing it, he scooted back as fast as he could. No shots were fired. He pulled bullets out rapidly and reloaded.

Gordon heard footsteps to his left. Johnson heard them also and pulled his gun to his shoulder, his helmet falling off as he moved. Then, with the quick thud of a round, the side of Johnson's head pushed out. Blood and brains flowed, spilling down to his shoulder. The footsteps stopped, leaving an awful silence.

"Oh, no," Gordon heard an American voice start to cry. "Jesus Christ, no, God, please, please, no. Fucking, no!"

One of the shadows ran past Gordon, falling to his knees and sobbing over Williams, upper body convulsing until he threw up. The other went to Johnson, dropped his rifle, fell to his knees and held what was left of Johnson's head in his lap. The truck got to the post, turned right quickly and sped away.

"No, no, come back – come back," the first shadow screamed. Many shadows crossed the field and arrived at the scene.

"Call the lieutenant," someone shouted. "Call the fucking lieutenant." In a few moments, a smaller figure approached.

"Quiet down," was the order. "What happened?"

"Friendly fire," someone yelled back. "Friendly fucking fire. We killed our own!"

A quick recounting of the previous moments followed.

"Two over here, two over there—four dead...friendly fucking fire. We killed our own, killed our fucking own."

It was the man holding Johnson's head, stroking it as if comforting a sick pet. "I knew him from high school, from high school," he cried, rocking the dead soldier in his lap. "This is Roy Johnson; he married my sister."

"Get him away from that soldier." The order was given in a voice cracking from emotion. Three other shadows ran over to him.

No, I won't let him go." He was scratching at the dirt, trying to pick up pieces of Johnson's head. He screamed again. "Leave me the fuck alone; let me be with him. Don't you realize? I just killed my brother-in-law."

"Get him away from the soldier." The voice no longer cracked.

Three men pulled the hysterical soldier to his feet.

"Jesus Christ, get him sedated. Call the medics in here. Now, fucking *now*." "Search the area." Same voice giving orders. "Make sure we have everyone accounted for, dead or alive." Twelve soldiers split up in pairs to start searching.

"This one," a soldier said, pointing to Williams, "seemed to be crawling toward him." He pointed to Johnson's dead body.

"Or away from him." A redheaded soldier with a deep Southern accent gestured at Gordon, who had started crawling out of the hole he was in.

"Oh, no, not another. That means five; we have five dead now."

"No, this one is still alive, barely. Get some medics in here now. We're not losing another," the lieutenant said sternly.

"Where's he hit?"

"Looks like both legs got tore up pretty bad; lost a lot of blood. Where the fuck are the medics?"

There was the sound of a quickly approaching vehicle bouncing over the holes, rocks and pits in the battlefield, doors opening and shutting, footsteps, more doors, and men running.

"Medics, over here!"

"What happened?"

"This one here is alive; save him."

The air was cloudy, foggy in the rising sun. Gordon felt hands on his legs, heard sighs and soft sobs from the men clustered around him. He recognized Johnson and Williams, standing in full dress uniform.

TWO

A warm, sunlit afternoon flooded central Arizona; there was not a cloud in the sky. Cindy sat in her living room, reading the paper and never noticing the car pull up out front. A firm knock on the front door startled her; she jumped and saw a uniformed figure through the window near the front door.

Fear froze her. She hadn't heard from her husband, Corporal Roy Johnson, in days, and she did not want to answer the door. As a second knock sounded, she reacted by bending forward, hands together, fingers entwined.

"Please, no," she begged in a desperate whispered prayer, not knowing if she had the strength to stand up. Her daughter, Carol, ran to the door.

"Daddy!" Carol sounded jubilant.

Cindy was confused; Roy was not due for rotation for at least four months. *Maybe Carol is just confusing the uniform,* she thought, keeping her hands together while lowering her head at the sound of the opening front door and hard shoes on the tile floor.

"Hi, Daddy! What are you doing home?"

Roy walked into the living room, holding his daughter.

"Oh, God, thank you!" Cindy ran to her husband.

He looked wonderful: uniform sharply pressed, ribbons properly in place, brass buttons and buckles brightly polished, even his shoes shined to a mirrored finish. Cindy threw her arms around him, sobbing and laughing at the same time. They embraced; he felt warm and solid. Carol put her arm around her mom and dad, and everything seemed familiar and right. They walked into the living room.

"Why didn't you tell me?" Cindy asked. "This is a wonderful surprise but I would have met the plane, would have waited all night and day for you." She kissed him. He smiled and kissed Carol, then buried his face in his wife's shoulder and shook a little. Cindy never knew Roy to show this type of emotion. The sound of car doors closing caught her attention.

"I'll see who it is," Carol said. Roy put his daughter on the ground and she ran to the front door.

"More soldiers," Carol announced.

Cindy looked at her husband questioningly and followed Carol to the front door. Two military men walked toward the house, solemn, heads high, faces serious. As they approached the door, one of them addressed her by name.

"Mrs. Johnson?"

They were dressed neatly. Not full dress, but still sharp, right down to the polished buttons.

"Yes."

"I'm Lieutenant Vincent Russo; this is Lieutenant Frank Muller. May we step in?"

"Sure." She opened the door, and Carol stepped back.

"You may need to sit down," Lieutenant Russo told her.

"I am sure that I can stand; I'm very fine."

"Well, ma'am, we regret to inform you that your husband, Corporal Roy Johnson, was killed in action."

"I think you've made a mistake," Cindy said quietly but confidently. "My husband just came home. He's standing in the living room."

"Yes. Mr. Soldiers," Carol said, pulling one of them by the hand and leading him into the living room, "come see my daddy."

"Roy, come talk to these men," Cindy called out as she followed. There was no answer.

"Roy?" Cindy walked around the soldiers into the empty living room.

"He must have stepped into the bathroom to wash up or maybe the bedroom to change," Cindy explained.

The soldiers exchanged a glance.

Carol said, "I'll go get him, Mommy," and ran to the other end of the house. After a few seconds, she came back out. "He's not there, Mommy."

"Roy?" Cindy called out, walking from room to room. "Roy?" The phone rang, sounding very loud, out of place, almost urgent. Cindy walked over to it, pushing her red hair back behind her ear.

"Hello?" Cindy said. There was a pause as she heard the response.

"Jimmy ... you calling from ...? What? I really don't have time ... there are two soldiers here ... what is it Jimmy? Why are you crying?" After a long pause, Cindy's face lost all color. Lieutenant Russo ran to hold her.

"What? What? Oh, sweet Jesus, what did you do, Jimmy? No, no, no, it can't be. Roy was just here. Both Carol and I held him; I wept on his shoulders...What are you saying, Jimmy? You did what?"

"Ma'am," Russo said, "please sit down." Lieutenant Muller took the phone and spoke into it.

"We know; it's in the report...It's got to be the worst...My heart and prayers are with you, brother. Keep your head."

Carol watched her mother, wide-eyed, as Cindy sat down, confused. Lieutenant Muller pulled out an envelope from his jacket pocket, opened it and handed it to her. It was the official notification from the Department of Defense explaining the way Roy died: head trauma—caused by friendly fire.

"No, this is wrong. Jimmy is wrong. You all are wrong," she said, dropping the envelope as if it was dirty. "He *is* here; I'm telling you." She got up and walked through the house.

"Daddy's just teasing us, right, Mommy?" Carol suggested bravely as she followed her mother, who went through the entire house twice before giving up.

"I don't understand this," she said, trembling. "I swear to you he knocked on the door just a few moments before you did. He was standing here." She pointed to the living room rug. "He was holding us; we were happy together."

"Ma'am, we have people you can talk to who can help you through this." Russo touched her on the arm.

"No, he was just here," she screamed.

Lieutenant Russo pulled out a cell phone and made a call. Then he explained the situation.

"Someone will be right here," he told Muller. Cindy returned to pacing through the house, calling her husband's name.

***

Bill and Ruth Johnson were sitting in their home near Atlanta, Georgia, watching a report on the evening news about four servicemen killed in action by friendly fire.

"Friendly fire," Bill said gruffly, "what a terrible term." Ruth nodded.

There was a knock on the door.

"Who could that be, so close to dinner and such?" Ruth got up to answer it

"Roy," Ruth yelled. "What are you—Bill, Roy is here."

My son, Bill thought, is still overseas, not due home for months. And why here? He should be going home to Cindy and Carol.

Ruth opened the door and held her son, who returned his mother's hug firmly, holding on for what Bill thought was just a little too long.

"Roy," Bill exclaimed, "why didn't you tell us? We didn't think we'd see you for months. Have you seen Cindy and Carol?"

Keeping his arm around Ruth, Roy walked to his father and, with his other arm, held his dad close. He buried his face in his mother's shoulder and trembled a bit. Bill hadn't seen his son show emotions since he was in grade school.

Effects of war? The phone rang.

"I'll get it," Ruth said.

"Hi, Cindy, guess what. Roy is—" she said. "What's the matter, dear? Cindy, please stop crying … what … Jimmy who?"

"That is not possible, honey," Ruth said, trying to calm her daughter-in-law. "Roy is right here with us."

Ruth put her hand over the phone and explained things to Bill. "The Department of Defense is there. They claim Roy was killed in action. Her brother Jimmy called and told her he was the one who shot Roy—something about friendly fire."

"Jesus Christ Almighty," Bill exclaimed. "Tell her it's a goddamned mistake. He's here; he's fine."

"Cindy, Roy is here, honey; everything is fine." Ruth looked into the empty living room. She said to her husband, "Go get Roy. Let him talk to her; the poor girl is hysterical. She's telling me he was there with her and Carol before the Defense Department got there, and then he was gone."

"Roy," Bill called out. "Roy, come talk to your wife; seems the Army got things screwed up good this time."

Bill went through the living room to the front door.

"Roy?"

He searched through the whole house while Ruth was trying to calm Cindy down. Finally, he walked back to his wife, all the blood drained from his face.

"I can't find him," he said. "He's not here." He could hear Cindy's cries over the phone.

THREE

It was a usual wet day in Seattle, Washington. Dave Williams, Joe's brother, was opening his bar for the day. He'd stopped opening for lunch once he finally had to admit that it just wasn't profitable, so had taken to arriving mid-afternoon to set up for the evening. His regulars would often be waiting for him as he parked his car in front.

"Running late again, Davey." Jimmy Wilson was leaning against the brick building that housed David's tavern.

"Jimmy, Jimmy, Jimmy," Dave said, "you're always wanting me to open early." He was calling over his shoulder as he locked his car door.

"You should be open for lunch," Jimmy said.

"Why, so you could come here, run up a bigger tab, and then start asking me to open for breakfast?"

"Deficit spending—credit— makes the world go 'round, my boy," Jimmy responded.

Jimmy was an average size man with a huge belly—"regal," as one of the other regulars described him. He always wore a large, Western style wide brimmed hat, which obviously looked out of place on the cloudy, wet streets of Seattle. Dave always wanted to ask Jimmy when the last time was that he saw his shoes, but had decided just to let his customers stay his customers.

Dave walked over to the front door of the tavern and shook Jimmy's hand before turning the key in the lock. As he held the door, allowing Jimmy to go in first, he looked up the street. A soldier, in full dress uniform, was walking in the general direction of the bar. It made him think of Joe.

"I'll have my usual, 'bahkeep.'" Jimmy made a poor impression of a character on an Eighties sitcom.

"One beer, on credit," David said, pouring. "Seriously, Jimmy, you're going to have to settle up."

Jimmy pulled his wallet out of his pants and started counting out some bills. The door to the bar opened.

"Joe?" Dave called.

Jimmy turned to look.

"A war hero comes home," Jimmy announced. "Get your butt over here and let me by you a beer," he said, handing Dave a wad of cash.

Dave looked at Joe, not paying attention to the cash that was just placed on the bar. His brother was home without notice: no phone call, no e-mail, not even a letter. Joe walked quietly to the bar, smiling slightly, his eyes holding a faraway twinkle. Nearly running, Dave greeted his younger brother with a huge embrace. Jimmy seemed a little embarrassed, as if he was intruding, and just patted Joe on the back. The phone rang.

"I'll answer that for you," Jimmy said, reaching across the bar and picking up the receiver.

"Why didn't you tell someone you were coming home?"

Joe said nothing.

"What?" Jimmy spoke to someone on the phone. Dave looked over at his customer.

"Sure, sure, Mrs. Williams. Dave, it's your mother. She's very upset."

"Mom?" Dave said into the phone. "Mom, calm down … What is it? … I can't understand you." He spoke quickly. "What do you mean, you can't find Joe? He's here; he can't be in two places at once …What? The Department of Defense … No, he's not; there has to be some kind of mistake … Mom, please calm down. Calm down, Mom. Joe is standing right here; he just walked into the bar." Dave looked up, smiling, but did not see his brother.

"Jimmy, go check the men's room. The Defense Department just delivered word to my mom that Joe's been killed in action. He's got to talk to her to calm her down." "Ahhh, Joey," Jimmy said, still in his 'not even close' false accent, "you gotta come out and talk to your ma. The ahmy has you as dead. Leave it to the ahmy, eh, Joey?" Jimmy opened the door to the men's room. Empty. He walked back out to the front of the bar.

"He ain't there," Jimmy said. "There's no one in the men's room."

"Go check by the back door," Dave said, frustrated. "He's got to be around here somewhere." He turned back and talked into the phone. "We'll find him, Mom. I just hugged him. He looked fine in his dress uniform."

Jimmy checked the back door; it was dead bolted and needed a key to open it. He poked his head into the women's room: empty. Jimmy's smile started to leave his face; he rubbed the back of his neck as if trying to get rid of a chill. He walked back through to the front of the bar, hearing Dave still consoling his mother, and opened the front door, looking up and down the street as Dave watched. He looked in both directions once again before coming back inside, shaking his head.

"Mom, we can't find him," Dave said. Then, after a pause, he added, "It doesn't make sense, Mom. He was just here." His voice was cracking.

"Jimmy and I saw him. He cannot be dead … I just hugged him."

FOUR

There was a crowd around him in the medical unit, and at least two doctors were probing and working on his legs while a nurse wiped his forehead with a moist cloth. Other medical personnel watched and monitored vital signs, reacting to orders by either handing the doctors their requests or running into an adjoining room to gather the needed supplies. Gordon felt nothing, not even the moist cloth on his head. It was neither hot nor cold, wet nor dry. Nothing.

"You hang in there," said a man behind a surgical mask encouragingly.

Gordon was the feature attraction in this tent in the middle of someplace. He had no idea where he was and even less of an idea of how he got there other than that he figured they must have flown him in.

Small lights kept shining in his eyes, and someone asked him to blink. *Why would they be looking in my eyes and ears when they feel fine?*

The same questions were asked over and over again and he gave the same answer each time: "I don't know."

"Barely responsive," was the condition being relayed to someone at the other end of his body.

"How is Cindy?" Gordon finally asked.

"Who is Cindy, Sergeant?"

"Johnson's wife. How is Carol doing?"

"Who is Carol?"

"Johnson's daughter," he said impatiently. "They need to know he was there. Tell them he was there. And his parents, Ruth and Bill, need to know he was there."

"Calm down, Sergeant." A pair of pretty eyes looked at him over a surgical mask. "Who was there?"

"How is Mrs. Williams?" Gordon croaked out.

"She's hysterical," came the reply.

"Mrs. Williams?" Pretty Eyes questioned.

"Yes, let her know that Joe *was* in her home and his brother's bar; tell her I saw him." Gordon saw someone injecting something in the IV he was connected to and he started feeling weaker and drowsier.

"No, don't," he said. "I need to tell them … they were …" He struggled to stay awake. Looking at a two paned window off to his right, he saw the faces of Roy Johnson and Joe Williams waving at him, giving him the thumbs up.

A nurse with no surgical mask greeted him. "Sergeant, how are you feeling this afternoon?" She lifted his head and gave him some water to sip through a straw.

"My legs?" he whispered.

"Can you feel them?"

He nodded and she smiled.

"They're still with you," she said reassuringly, "but I should let the doctors explain. Let me go get one of them." She let his head down gently and walked quickly away from the bed.

He was no longer in the tent. There was no window to his right, no Johnson and Williams' reassuring thumbs up. He was in a medical ward filled with beds pushed against dull white walls that lined both sides of a long narrow room.

Some of the beds did not have any sheets, exposing bare, striped, thin mattresses. There were some occupied beds barely out of view behind a cloth divider, beds containing what was left of young men hooked up to machines handling various functions that their bodies once did, including breathing.

Each machine had its own noise, beep, or hiss, making the ward sound like a small musical group warming up for an evening concert. The nurse returned, following a short, round man in a long white coat with dark stubble on his face.

"Sergeant, it's good to see you awake." The man in the white coat spoke clearly, though with a slight Spanish accent. "I'm Doctor Sierra. How are you feeling?"

"Pretty good, now that I saw her again," he said, pointing to the nurse standing alongside of him. Both the nurse and the doctor laughed too hard.

"Well, that is a good sign. But let me explain what is going on with you," the doctor said. "Those bullets tore you up pretty good." He removed some of the bandages as he explained. "We were not sure at first if we were going to be able to save either leg."

As Gordon listened he saw another woman, one with very long black hair, walking quickly up the ward toward them. "But we were lucky," the doctor continued. "Well, you and we were both lucky that we had a surgeon visiting us that day who had a lot of experience in saving extremities." The image of Johnson and Williams' thumbs up came into his mind. "Doctor Springer will explain the rest."

The woman with the long black hair stepped to the other side of the bed. She smiled warmly, adjusted her white coat, and introduced herself.

"Elaine Springer," she said. Her eyes were bright and clear. "You were fortunate to keep your legs, Gabriel. Even though there was significant damage, we were able to connect enough blood vessels and tissues to save them."

"Will I be able to walk?"

"Recoveries from leg injuries are tricky, and no one knows for sure how it will go or how much use you will get back," she said, stroking the bottom of one of his feet, which promptly twitched.

"*That* is a good sign," Dr. Sierra said. "You felt that?"

"My feet are very ticklish; always have been," Gordon said.

Dr. Springer continued, "Any sensation or feeling is a great sign, but we are not sure how much use you will have. There are just too many variables. You may make a full recovery or you may need a wheelchair. Those are the best and worst case scenarios."

"Let's go for the full recovery," Gordon said.

The pretty nurse stepped to the front of the bed. "That is where I come in," she said.

He smiled. "There is a God." He put his hands together as if in prayer, looking at the ceiling. Both doctors laughed. It seemed to be a laugh of relief.

Dr. Springer walked over to the nurse. "Nurse Savard is our physical therapist. She will help you while you are here. Remember, I said help. This recovery is yours; she can only instruct, assist, and observe."

"Nancy Savard." The nurse introduced herself, extending a hand. .

"How long have I been here?"

"A fairly long time. More than ten days," Dr. Springer explained. "You are in Germany, at the best hospital in Europe."

"Germany," Gordon exclaimed. "How long? When?"

"You were airlifted off the battlefield two weeks ago."

"Two weeks?" Gordon could not comprehend the amount time that had passed.

Nurse Savard stepped up again. "Yes, two weeks," she affirmed, looking at the doctors who took a half step back. "You lost a lot of blood; you could barely answer questions at the field hospital. That is when Dr. Springer started working on you"

"You were there also, Nurse Savard," Dr. Springer confirmed.

"Yes, I was there," Nurse Savard agreed. "I was the one wiping your forehead."

"I remember, the pretty eyes."

"Sergeant," Nurse Savard asked, "who are Johnson and Williams?"

"Why?" He remembered seeing them and telling people to reassure the families. But he didn't know if he was recalling a dream or something he'd really said.

"You were talking about them on the operating table," Nurse Savard responded. "You even said they waved to you from the window."

Gordon took a deep breath. Nurse Savard held his hand firmly and put her other hand on his shoulder.

"They are my men, served under me. We were pinned down the night my legs were hurt. They did what they could to stop the bleeding, found a place for me to stay, and waited with me all night long," Gordon explained.

The nurse nodded and then asked, "Who is Cindy?"

"Johnson's wife. He also has a daughter named Carol." Tears started filling his eyes. "Are they all right? Do they believe he was there?"

Nurse Savard bent over, whispering in his ear "Sergeant, you do know that Roy Johnson is dead."

"Yes. Friendly fire." Gordon was weeping hard. "But he was there, in their home, in their living room. He held them both one last time. They must believe that."

Dr Sierra spoke up. "You need rest."

"And Joe Williams," Gordon continued, "he was at his brother's bar in Seattle and also with his mother. Dave and his mom need to know. Joe was there, in both places."

"Okay, okay," Dr. Sierra spoke up again. "Enough for now. You need rest."

Gordon rubbed the tears from his eyes. Nurse Savard was still holding his hand. Dr. Springer looked one last time at the bandages. "You may need some additional surgery, but we will make that decision as we go along."

The two doctors walked away.

"My folks?" Gordon inquired, looking at Nurse Savard. "Do they know? Are they aware?"

"Yes," she said. "We have been in constant touch with them. They have all the up to date information. We'll get a phone in here in a little while so you can talk with them."

"What time is it?" Gordon asked. "Pop is usually in bed by nine, and there's a seven hour time difference with Germany."

"Yes, its seven hours later here, so you should be fine," she said. "And I've talked with your dad, so my guess is he won't mind if you wake him up this one time. But you could wait 'til morning."

"Nurse," Dr. Sierra called from the other end of the ward, beckoning. She went to answer his summons, but returned in moments.

"It seems the decision has been made for you. Your dad's on the phone now, and we should have it all set up to get a phone to you any minute," she told him. "Sometimes these things just work out by themselves."

Thirty seconds later, two soldiers entered the ward, one carrying large loops of wire and the other carrying a phone. "Welcome, Sergeant," one of them said. "How're you feeling?"

"Fine. How about you?"

"Never better, Sergeant, and we're all glad you are here." He handed Gordon the phone.

"Hello," Gordon said. He heard his father breathe in and then start to cry.

"Take it easy, Pop. Yeah, I understand." He could barely distinguish what his father was saying over the sobs and laughter. "I'm okay. Yeah, a little banged up but still in one piece. Sure, I bet you were scared, but don't get mad at me; they just told me I've been sleeping for two weeks. You hated to have me sleep past eight a.m."

His father laughed hard, occasionally sobbing, while telling Gordon the whole time he was unconscious that he felt he never told him enough how much he loved him. He was so afraid he would not get the chance to make it up.

"I would have called, Pop," he said through his own tears, "but, ya know, this damned Army won't let any phone calls go out with unauthorized objects imbedded in its property." Gordon was trying to joke about the bullets in his legs keeping him from making a call "Yeah, Pop, a two-week drunk is one way to put it, but it was a party I never want to see again."

"Yeah, Mom ... now take it easy. You know you get me crying when you cry. Mom. Mom? There are men here, you know ... I do have my rank to consider... They don't promote girly men." Gordon broke down.

Nurse Savard stayed close by during the conversation. She appeared busy but was really closely monitoring her patient.

After a few moments, Gordon composed himself and explained what happened, piecing things together from what he remembered and what had been told to him. "I don't remember all the shots that hit me, but I do remember the men I was with and how they protected me and got me to safety. And then I saw them killed ... friendly fire. Yeah, I know, it's a horrible term. But I never want to forget Johnson and Williams ... Roy and Joe. Why you asking, Pop? Where?"

His father said that two soldiers in full dress uniform stayed with them the night he was in surgery. They came to the front door and introduced themselves as men who served with him, then stayed through those long hours of the operation until the hospital called to say Gordon was out of danger and things looked promising. When his parents tried to give the news to Johnson and Williams, they were gone.

"Are you sure it was Roy Johnson and Joe Williams?" Gordon asked. "Yes, I know they are fairly common names."

It was very quiet on the phone. Nurse Savard walked over to him; he put up one finger to her and spoke with his parents. "Sure, Mom, I'll call in a couple of days. Dad, I am okay. You got to believe that. You should see the nurse that's going to help me walk again. Like I told the doctors, there is a God. Love you, too." He handed the phone to the nurse. She signaled the soldiers at the other end of the ward. They rolled up the wire, nodded to the sergeant, and left.

"So, that was a good call. Sometimes tears, even tears from a hardnosed, ranking sergeant, can help," she said, with a teasing smile.

"Yeah."

"Over the next few weeks, we will be talking about many things, Sergeant," she said, matter of factly.

"Please, call me Gabe. It's short for Gabriel."

"I like that name."

"I remember dreaming that before the Department of Defense gave the news to Johnson's wife and daughter, Roy was there. He held them close, not saying anything."

"That is Cindy and Carol, right?"

"Yes. Roy also visited his parents in my dream."

"But this felt more real than a dream," she said.

"Sure did."

"I also remember dreaming that Joe Williams visited his brother's bar in Seattle before his mother called with the news that Joe was killed in action. She was hysterical because Joe had been with her before the DOD arrived."

"I've heard stories like this before." She was trying to comfort him.

He continued explaining, still trying to make sense of it all. "Now, my parents told me that during the night I was operated on two soldiers in full dress uniform were with them, comforting them all those hours while I was in danger. Then they were gone as soon as word reached my parents that things with me had improved. They introduced themselves as Roy Johnson and Joe Williams."

"We will have plenty of time to talk about these things."

"Nurse Savard, right," he smiled at her. "I was just explaining to my parents about God."

"I heard, and my name is Nancy."

FIVE

Lights went out in the ward at ten p.m. Gabriel was not sleepy, so he lay staring at the ceiling, listening to the mechanical beeping, clicking, and hissing from the various machines at the far end of the ward that blended roughly with the occasional coughing and snoring of the other patients. His mind wandered.

Johnson and Williams visited my parents while I was being operated on. They comforted them. They protected me while on the battlefield. What am I supposed to make of that? Friendly fire. How did it all go so wrong? How are the men who shot them coping? I heard their cries when they discovered the bodies, their screams, their guilt. Who were the men who died on the other side of the battlefield that night?

The gray German morning came up slowly after the long sleepless night. A different doctor was in the ward this morning.

"I'm Doctor Moore," he said. "How did you sleep, Sergeant?" He looked at the chart hanging at the foot of the bed.

"Not well. I guess after sleeping for two weeks I didn't really feel tired."

The doctor lifted up the bandages on his legs. "Can you feel this?"

Gabriel jumped.

"Ticklish?"

Gabriel nodded.

"You'll probably get some rehab work today."

"From Nurse Savard?" Gabriel nodded enthusiastically as he asked the question.

"She's the one," he said. "By the way, your smile makes it too obvious."

"After what I've been through," Gabriel responded, "the hell with the rules."

"I am not sure, but I think you are giving good signs." Dr. Moore smiled.

He walked toward the nurse, who was working with another patient, pausing to say something to her. Gabriel returned her smile when she looked his way. She stayed a few more minutes, working with the soldier, then she made a note on his chart before walking over to Gabe.

"Good morning, Gabe," she said. "Dr. Moore just told me that you don't hold to a lot of rules right now." She looked very serious.

"At this point," Gabriel told her, "the only rules I want are the ones that make me feel better." He raised his hands to his face and seemed surprised that it was almost fully bearded. "Geesh, when did I grow my face?"

"Looks like about two weeks' growth. How's that for not obeying the rules?" she said. "We'll get you propped up so you can shave."

"Okay," he responded. "But he did say something—the doctor did—about starting some therapy?"

"We should start to get your legs muscles moving," she noted, moving down alongside the bed by his legs. "It won't be much at first, and, for the next year or so, your legs will be very sore, sometimes painful."

"Year?"

"Maybe longer," Nancy said seriously. "You had very serious injuries." She lifted the bandages, checking the wounds. "Let's start with some lifts."

She put her hand under his ankle and calf, raising them just a few inches. A pain shot up his leg. Seeing this, she quickly but gently lowered the leg.

"That hurt," Gabriel said through his teeth.

"I know. It was probably a combination of stretching the wounds and sutures, plus using muscles that have been severely damaged."

She positioned her hands again and lifted him. It hurt, once again, but this time Gabriel was able to feel the difference between stretching the sutures and the wounds as well as the muscles.

"So, tell me more about Johnson and Williams," Nancy chatted while watching his leg movements.

"What do you mean?"

"You said they put you in a protected area. Do you remember how you got hurt?" "We were on patrol at night, walking up a street, when we heard shots up ahead. Johnson was in the rear, watching for anything that could come up behind us. When I sent Williams up ahead to scout the gunfire, Johnson moved up. We stood back to back, watching."

Nancy moved her attention to the other leg, placing her hands under it in the same manner as the first and lifted just a few inches. The pain that shot up his leg was as bad as the first one had been. Gabriel grimaced.

"You were saying, Gabe?"

"I was?" He was trying to make a joke about the pain, but even he did not think it was funny. His legs really hurt. "Okay, so after about thirty seconds, Williams comes back and says some of our guys have the enemy pinned down two blocks up. I asked him if he thought they needed help; he didn't know. The three of us decided to assist and started moving ahead to the firefight."

The lifts and movement Nancy was applying to his legs, though still painful, were becoming easier and smoother.

"We made it to the corner, with Johnson still watching the rear while I went to find the officer in charge. Johnson yelled out and started firing. Williams and I spun around, observing enemy reinforcements quickly coming up behind us. It seemed, by following at a distance, they were coming to the fight and using us as cover.

"Once they realized we saw them, they opened fire, pinning us down. I ran to a vehicle nearby for cover, returning fire while I did so. I went down—my right ankle hurting badly. Williams told me I had been hit. I saw the blood on my shoe and tried to walk but I couldn't."

Nancy lowered the leg and then checked the bandages. There was a red spot spreading on the front of the leg she last worked on.

"Let me check that," she said. "What happened next? You were hit in more than just the ankle."

"Williams put my arm around his shoulder and helped me up. We headed for the nearest building, with bullets flying all around us. I was trying to help as much as possible, but my ankle was bleeding badly and I couldn't put any weight on it. Johnson came up behind us, returning fire in the direction we were receiving.

"We made it to a building and, as we went through the door, Williams tripped, dumping me out on the ground outside. I started crawling, using only my arms. I got myself to what I thought was just about all the way in the building, not realizing my legs were still outside the door. I heard gunfire, and then felt my legs get shot up pretty good. Johnson hit the door about this time, jumping in. He and Williams pulled me the rest of the way in."

"How did you get to the field?"

"It was a hell of a firefight, with bullets coming in from all over. I swore at the time they were coming at us through the wall and the ceiling. The three of us flattened out on the floor as best as we could. Using just my arms again, I pulled myself over near a window, which provided a good view of the street. There must have been twenty of the enemy outside, firing round after round into the building we were in. I propped myself up against the wall and started firing back while Williams worked on my legs, just trying to control the bleeding."

"What he did," she said, "probably saved your legs—and your life."

Her statement caught him off guard. He realized Williams had saved his life, but hadn't considered his legs.

"Johnson repeatedly called out in the street for a medic, firing blindly before and after each call. But no one answered. Somewhere nearby I heard one of our guys talking, probably on a radio or a phone, giving location and coordinates. He was almost screaming. He kept saying hurry, hurry, hurry.

"The shooting kept up. We gave as good as we got, all three of us pouring bullets through that one open window. We all knew they had to get me out of there. Williams pointed to a rear door and both of them grabbed one of my arms, lifted me, and ran out."

Nancy was almost finished replacing the bandages, making them a little tighter, which also hurt.

"So, if I'm feeling pain, is that a good sign?"

"Not necessarily," she said with a serious face.

He continued, "Once through the door, we were on the edge of an open field. I could still hear the firefight going on behind us and footsteps all around. They dragged me along the side of the building, back in the direction we came from, with shots ringing out, hitting the wall and ricocheting in all directions. We fell into the ditch of what was left of an old bombed-out building. They covered me with debris, leaving an opening for me to see from and telling me not to move.

"I heard a tank move into the street we'd just left. After couple of loud explosions, everything went quiet. No more shooting. Williams kept coming back to check my legs and slow the bleeding. We must have been there for an hour before they tried to get the attention of a truck that came up in field."

"So your wounds were not from friendly fire?"

"Impossible to tell; shots were coming from everywhere. Johnson and Williams were definitely friendly fire." His voice started to break, and rubbed a tear from his eye.

Nancy pulled up a chair and sat down. "We'll get you propped up in a while, and shaved, although I kind of like beards." She winked. "Tell me again about Johnson's wife and what you saw."

"I was probably dreaming." Gabriel looked away.

"Tell me anyway."

He described the scene of Johnson's reunion with his family, his voice cracking as he relieved watching them hold each other.

"Did he say anything to them?"

It was only then, with Nancy's question, did he realize that Johnson never said anything—not a word, not even a greeting. He'd just smiled, picked up his daughter and walked in, greeting his wife with a hug.

"He held them like he never wanted to let go … it was a dream." Gabriel shook his head like he was trying to clear it. "Johnson loved to talk but didn't in the dream, not even to his family. It *had* to be a dream."

"How about at his parents' place?"

"No, he didn't say anything there, either."

"And Williams?"

"You remember this stuff better than I do," Gabriel joked. "No, Joe was quiet. He was not much of a talker, though he did love his brother's bar. When he did talk about home, he said his first stop would be at his brother's bar because he was going to drink up his brother's profits for the whole time he spent in war. But when he walked in that bar, all he did was look at his brother and smile. Just like Johnson did with his family."

Nancy listened intently.

"Why are you so interested?" he asked her.

"I guess, Gabe," she said, skirting the subject, "that even though I am a sucker for a well-groomed beard, you need to follow the rules on this one. Let's prop you up." She flashed a bright smile while pulling a rolling frame over to the bed. It had a triangle hanging from a single overhead bar.

"You pull, I'll lift," she directed, putting her arms around his chest and holding him. Gabriel reached up and lifted himself, pulling his legs further up toward the head of the bed. Nancy smelled nice, he realized.

"You stink pretty," he told her.

"Thank you." She laughed, and then frowned. "Besides a shave, you could use a bath."

"Oh, Nurse Savard," he whined, "I don't think I have the strength."

"Well, Sergeant, if that is the case, let me see if I can get one of these male orderlies to sponge you down," she retorted.

"Give me a minute," Gabriel said, taking a deep breath. "I think I just regained my strength."

Nancy handed him a small scissor and razor, then pushed over a tray that had some soap, water, and an upright mirror on it.

"I'll check on you later," she said. He watched her walk out of the ward.

The mirror did not display a comforting image. He looked at his reflection, failing to recognize himself. He looked older than twenty-four—much older.

"Sergeant Gordon?" he heard.

Gabriel looked around. The nearest bed had a soldier in a body wrap, including the head. He was in traction, with both legs in the air.

"Sergeant Gabriel Gordon?" The question was coming from the soldier in the body wrap.

"That's me," Gabriel responded.

"I'm Corporal Allan Paul."

"Good to know you, Corporal."

"Sergeant, what were you explaining to Nurse Savard?"

"How I got wounded."

"There was more to it than that, Sergeant."

"Oh, you mean the dreams? Those were about my men's family and stuff."

"Would you describe your men?"

Gabriel spent a few seconds describing both Roy Johnson and Joe Williams, what they'd looked like, the way they'd talked and laughed. It made him feel good to remember them that way.

"Was Johnson a big man with a scar on his left cheek?"

Gabriel paused before answering. Johnson got that scar in a firefight six months earlier. It wasn't a serious wound, nothing to keep him out of action; just enough that he'd carry the reminder. "Do I know you from some place, Allan? Did you serve with Johnson and me?"

"This is the only place we've served together, Sergeant."

Gabriel was uncomfortable, not really wanting to ask the next question. But he wanted the answer. "How did you know about Johnson's scar?"

"When you were brought in here, there were two soldiers in full dress standing by your bed each night. One was very tall and had a scar."

"Each night?"

"Yes, Sergeant. As soon as lights went out, they stood on either side of you all night long, in full dress uniform and at attention."

"Were they here last night?"

"Yes. When you started stirring the night before, not fully awake but finally showing movement, they relaxed but kept standing by you. They did the same thing last night. One of them or both of them were always here."

Three beds away, an older soldier propped himself up on one elbow. "I saw them, too," he said.

"Every night?" Gabriel asked again.

"All night long, at attention, until you became conscious," he said "Then at ease after that."

"I think we're all having the same dream," Gabriel told them.

A soldier on the other end of the ward sat up in bed, pulled over his crutches, got up, and made his way toward Gabriel's bed. He had only one leg; the white bandaged stump moved in rhythm with his striding crutches. He extended his hand as he reached the sergeant's bed.

"I'm Lieutenant Dan Stiles," he introduced himself.

"Good to know you, sir," Gabriel responded, shaking his hand.

"Sir? Don't call me sir, Sergeant. In here, I am just as good as you are," he said, making Gabriel laugh. "It is not a dream, Sergeant," he went on. "Each one of us has had these things happen. That's one of the reasons we're together."

"We're not here because we're wounded?" Gabriel teased.

"No," the lieutenant said. "I don't know why they're grouping us together, but they are very interested in our stories." He stood at the foot of Gabriel's bed, turning toward a man the bed across from him.

"Jeff Baker, would you like to go first?"

"My unit was led through a province held by enemy combatants," Baker began. "We were told they were the most battle-experienced of the enemy and we were to expect the worst if it came to a combat. We had orders at the start of our patrol to check out every structure in a small village that appeared to be deserted. It had about twelve small buildings.

"We checked out the first two and found nothing. Rodriguez took the lead into the third building, and we heard some footsteps coming from the back. Harris and I headed around back and took out the first two we saw running away. Then more footsteps came from inside. Harris and I entered the back of the structure. Shots were fired; Harris was hit in the face and dropped."

Baker's voice started shaking. "I hit the floor and rolled, returning the fire. Then I heard what sounded like a body fall. Rodriguez called out to me, saying he was okay. I told him Harris was down and reached out to Harris to check for a pulse. Then I told Rodriguez that Harris had 'bought' it. I heard Rodriguez moan. We heard more footsteps, this time running outside. I looked out a window and saw an enemy with an RPG launcher aimed directly for our building." His voice was getting anxious.

"I screamed and hit the ground. There was an explosion. The ceiling caved in, and Rodriquez screamed. That's the last I remember." Baker's bandaged hand pointed to his body. "The explosion must have caused a fire because I suffered third degree burns on more than thirty-five percent of my body and was unconscious for over four weeks."

"You gonna be okay?" Gabriel asked.

"Surgeries are going to start in a few weeks—back home." He continued, "While I was unconscious, I saw both Rodriguez and Harris visit their families, like you said, getting there just before notification of next of kin. They held their wives, kids, and parents one more time, then disappeared once the notification arrived."

He paused a moment and then went on. "My mom told me, when I first spoke with her after I woke up, that every evening two soldiers would sit with her for a few moments just before she got the daily update on my condition. They hardly spoke, but she said their names were Rodriguez and Harris. After she got the word I was going to make it, she never saw them again."

"Okay," Gabriel said. "We've all heard these kinds of ghost stories before. The Army probably has us together for some kind of study in mass hysteria or hallucinations. After all, we're awake."

"But," Lieutenant Stiles interrupted, "we're not seeing just our own embrace their loved ones." He looked at the soldier propped up on one elbow.

"I'm Private Washington."

For some reason, it was only when he said his name that Gabriel realized he was black. The private then shared his story.

"My firefight was similar to Baker's. I was caught in a building under rocket-propelled grenade attack. The place was a shambles—ceilings falling, walls tumbling—though I was well protected and still had a good view of the enemy.

"I saw that each time he shot, he would have to open himself up a bit, standing up over a small waist high wall," Washington continued. "He must have been assisted by someone, because he popped up to shoot, and then ducked behind the wall. He'd be back quickly to pop back up again and shoot. There was no way he could have reloaded that fast by himself. He must have had two launchers and someone reloading.

"So I aimed in the area he was popping up, timing his movement. He popped up, I fired, he fired, he dropped. The RPG hit right under me and that's the last I remember."

"And did you dream?" Gabriel asked.

He nodded and then resumed his story. "There was a small village, I'm not sure where, but it hadn't been touched by the war. The buildings were dusty but everything else was complete and intact. I walked through this village, watching children playing and mothers talking. No one noticed me.

"There was a man in front of a small house. He wore a tattered uniform and was knocking on the door. He banged quite a few times before a woman inside answered, almost complaining. I couldn't understand the language but it sounded like she was really bitching out whoever was at the door.

"When she opened the door, her eyes went wide in recognition. She threw her arms around the man, crying. They held each other for quite some time.

"There was some commotion on the road behind me, and I turned to see some old pickup truck, with the bed wide open, coming down the road into the village. The villagers gasped and moaned as they walked down the road alongside this truck, pointing toward the end of the village to little house where I stood.

"The trucks started moving faster down the center of the village and eventually stopped near me. I could see there was someone lying in the bed of the truck.

"The woman let go of the man and walked to the street. Another woman met her halfway and tried to hold her back, attempting to keep her away from the truck. She pushed the women aside and went to the truck, her eyes opening in shock. She put her hand to her chest, shaking her head no, and pointed back to her house. The man was gone."

Silence followed Private Washington's story. The others' stories had involved people who had served together and seemingly reached out to loved ones to say goodbye as they crossed over. But Washington's story was not about seeing the people he served reaching out. It was about seeing someone from the enemy reaching out to his loved ones, someone he did not know; someone he was there to kill.

Lieutenant Stiles was still sitting on the foot of the sergeant's bed when he started to tell his story. "I was leading two patrols into an airport. It was a small airport but suspected as being part of a supply line allowing weapons into the area each evening. Our job was to set up hidden points to watch and intercept. I had Jim Billings, a sergeant with two tours in the area, on my left, and Billy Smith, a first tour corporal, on my right. We were set up pretty tight in a hangar at the leading edge, closest to the runway. Everything, planes and vehicles, had to pass that spot.

"An enemy patrol came into the hangar, and it looked like they were getting set up to unload a plane. I nodded at Billings and Smith, and we opened fire, taking out everyone in that patrol. Two more enemy patrols remained just outside and answered our fire with theirs. They entered in front of us and behind us. Billings bought it first. Smith second. I felt a sharp pain in my leg," Stiles reached down to where his leg used to be. "and that is the last I remember."

"Each night when the lieutenant first came here," Washington said, "there were two men matching the descriptions of Billings and Smith standing by his bed. Billings' father contacted me here. Nurse Savard stood by me while I talked on the phone. I was still pretty weak. It was tough to talk to his dad. He told me how his Jimmy visited him just before the DOD knocked on the door."

"Tell him about Smith," Stiles interjected.

"Very similar to your story, Sergeant," Allan said. "Smith visited his family just before the DOD gave notification. His wife, Jean, had to be sedated. She swore that Smith was still alive. Everyone who comes in this ward has similar stories."

"The people on other wards don't have stories or such experiences?" Gabriel asked.

Dan shrugged his shoulders. "Maybe, but we're more seriously wounded."

"But we have heard rumors that, in the other wards, there are soldiers standing by the side of some of the more emotionally wounded," Washington added.

"Why?" Gabriel asked. "Why would they seem to be keeping this in one place?"

Nancy came into the ward and walked directly to the group of men. "What is this, a union meeting?" she asked jokingly.

"No unions allowed in the Army," the lieutenant quipped back.

She walked check Allan's bandages as Dan went back to his bed. She injected something into Allan's IV and then walked over to Washington, giving him a pill and a glass of water to help him swallow. He took the pill and finished the cup of water in two gulps.

She checked Dan's bandages and then removed them. His stump was badly discolored; the purple sutures still visible and angry looking. She cleaned the stump tenderly, going over the same area lightly, obviously trying to avoid causing discomfort. She re-bandaged the leg and propped the lieutenant's pillow behind his head. Then she walked over to Gabriel.

"You need to sleep, Sergeant," she said with a smile.

"I'm not tired."

"Rest will help heal those legs," she said. She handed Gabriel a pill and then went to the other end of the ward to get a cup of water.

Gabriel put the pill under his tongue and drank the water, then handed her back the cup. Once she left, Gabriel spit out the pill and slipped it under the sheet. After a short while, he pretended to be asleep.

SIX

Lying sleepless in bed, Cindy could still feel Roy's arms around her, just as they were before the DOD knocked on the door. Some days she found herself walking around the house, calling his name; she was so sure he was still around. Carol also wanted to know what happened to her daddy. Many times the little girl said, "But, Mommy, he was right here."

Cindy had no explanation, and she wanted one. She started researching apparitions, visitations from the dead, and found some comfort in the stories of how the deceased made contact with loved ones at the moment they passed over. But none had the physical connection that she and Carol experienced. Instead, most of the stories related seeing a shadow and hearing a song, or a book falling open to a certain sentence or passage that the deceased loved.

The two soldiers who delivered the news of Corporal Roy Johnson's death had repeated Cindy's experience to their commanders, who in turn notified Chaplain Lance Kirkland. When he called, she agreed to meet with him.

"Roy was in my arms; he was holding Carol and me in our living room," Cindy explained.

"Did he say anything?"

"No, he just held us."

"Before he came to the door, when was the last time you heard from him?"

"Two nights before," Cindy answered. "We spoke by cell phone."

"Where was he?"

"With his unit."

"Did he say he was coming home?"

"No, he still had four months to go on his tour."

"What did you think when he showed up?"

"Other than being surprised," she smiled, "I thought he knew when we spoke that he was going to be home but was trying to keep it a surprise."

"How was he dressed?"

"In full dress uniform," she responded. "Medals and all."

"Is that the way he usually dressed when he came home?"

"No; he usually wore his fatigues."

"How did he appear to his parents?"

"The same way. Full dress."

"Did he say anything to them?"

"No, he didn't say a word. He just hugged them both. He walked in a few seconds before I called them."

"It says here," the chaplain said, "that his body will be coming home this afternoon."

"Yes," Cindy said, "and I'm going to meet it. I need to see him."

"You really up to that?"

"I need to see him."

The chaplain expressed his concern. "Mrs. Johnson, your husband suffered a severe head wound. A viewing could be quite traumatic. Are you sure you want to see it, to remember him that way?"

"I don't know what's worse, holding him, believing my senses that contradict what the government told me, or seeing him terribly wounded and dead," Cindy said tearfully. "Chaplain, which thought or memory would you want to live with the rest of your life?"

Chaplain Kirkland had handled many tough questions from grieving family members and loved ones before, but this one … what was the best of the two memories?

"I can't answer that, Mrs. Johnson. I just don't have the answer." Then, "May I accompany you this afternoon?"

Cindy broke down. "Yes," she said through a muffled sob. "I believe I will need that."

***

"Sir," the Chaplain's receptionist called out, "there's a call from Germany for you. Nancy Savard."

"Thank you," he said. "I'll take it."

He was surprised; while he knew Nancy, he hadn't heard from her in over two years. They'd served together on some joint NATO exercises in Bosnia and discussed "crossing over" stories often. She often expressed her frustration over his apparent resistance to the idea of the dead making contact.

"Nancy Savard, what a surprise," he said.

"Lance Kirkland," Nancy responded with the same formality. "How are you?"

"It's been over two years," he said. "I didn't think that you were still in the service."

"A calling is a calling."

She had never considered her military career a calling. While she was very capable, handling the most physically demanding and emotionally upsetting assignments with high efficiency and care, it was always a duty and not a calling.

"A calling." Kirkland sounded surprised. "Now that is new. Welcome to the club."

"That is why I am contacting you, Lance. We need to talk about something personal. Can I call you at home?"

"Sure," he replied, giving her his home info. "There's quite a time difference, eight hours or so."

"I'll stay up and call you around six p.m. your time."

SEVEN

The chaplain met Cindy at the airfield security office at the appointed hour. "Mrs. Johnson," he asked, "are you still okay to do this?" She nodded.

Kirkland walked over to the soldier in back of the office and spoke with him for a few minutes. The soldier picked up the phone, dialed, and then handed it to Kirkland. Cindy could tell the chaplain was explaining something at length to whoever was on the phone. He stopped talking for a long time, waiting on hold. After a few minutes he said a couple of words and handed the phone back to the soldier. He smiled and nodded to her as he walked back across the office.

"We will meet the plane," he said. "There are ceremonies and formalities involved in bringing the war dead home"

"I know," she said quietly, her eyes not meeting his.

"I just finished explaining to the base commander what you wanted and was able to arrange a special viewing for you. Your husband will be moved to an empty room in the hangar so you can have some private time."

"Thank you," she said, barely above a whisper.

"There is one other thing," Kirkland went on. "The base commander wants to be there."

Before she could respond, a side door in the security office opened quickly. A short, thin officer stepped through.

"Commander John Donner." The chaplain saluted and then introduced Cindy to the base commander. He reached to shake her hand.

"Mrs. Johnson, you have my deepest condolences," Donner said, holding Cindy's hand between his.

"Thank you."

"The chaplain explained what you've experienced, and I do understand your confusion. But are you sure you want to do this?"

Cindy straightened, her eyes narrowing a bit. "Yes. I need to see him."

The three of them rode together quietly to the hangar. The plane landed as they arrived. They got out of the car and stood near the hangar opening as the plane taxied toward them. It came to a stop few hundred feet away, engines slowly winding down to an unnatural and almost unwanted silence. The speaker systems in the hangar started playing "The Army Goes Rolling Along" almost gaily.

The commander moved quickly to a phone near the hangar door and the music stopped immediately. Kirkland put both arms around the weeping woman.

Eight soldiers, dressed as sharply as Roy Johnson was when he visited his family, walked slowly toward the plane. Marching in unison, their heels hit the tarmac at the same time, making an out of place, disturbing clicking sound. They timed their progress to arrive in position when the door to the plane had lowered completely to the ground. The soldiers lined up in two lines of four at the rear of the plane, faced each other and then became very still. Taps started playing over the loudspeakers and the soldiers respectfully brought their right arms up in a salute as the caskets were rolled slowly down the ramp on a black mechanical conveyor belt.

Sobs were heard over the music as, one by one, the flag draped coffins came down the ramp. The sound caused Cindy to turn. There was a long, three tiered grandstand at the far end of the hangar area where a small group of people stood watching the coffins descend.

Donner walked toward the plane. He stopped at the end of one of the lines of soldiers, adding his salute to each passing coffin. When all six caskets had descended the ramp, electric vehicles moved into place, their quiet movements adding to the solemnity of the moment.

After the last coffin came off the plane, Donner was handed a clipboard, which he checked. Then he spoke quietly to two of the soldiers, who placed a coffin on one of the vehicles. The two soldiers accompanied the vehicle, walking slowly on each side as the vehicle conveyed the coffin toward the hangar. Donner followed behind. When they reached the hangar opening, Donner signaled to Kirkland and Cindy.

They approached, the chaplain with his arm around Cindy, who shook with emotion as they stopped alongside the steel gray coffin that held the body of her husband. Donner motioned to the soldiers to escort the coffin to a room on the other side of the hangar. The vehicle moved ahead slowly.

Across the other side of the hangar was an open door that led to a lit room. Cindy saw a soldier in full dress uniform standing against the far wall of the room, with his hands behind him and his feet slightly apart. He came to attention as the coffin and escorts came within full view and walked across the room slowly, still at attention, eyes forward, hat under his right arm.

Cindy breathed in deeply as she saw him, and Kirkland once again put his arm around her. Donner quickened his steps to catch up with the soldiers and said something to one of them.

"I asked for this room to be unoccupied," Donner said.

"That is what we expected, sir."

"Then who is that soldier in the room?"

"I don't know, sir."

The soldier Donner spoke with walked into the room to get the cart that Johnson's coffin would be placed on, stopping momentarily to address the soldier standing at attention in the room.

"Who is he?" Donner asked, when the soldier who wheeled the cart came out of the room.

"I don't know, sir. He would not answer."

Donner entered into the room ahead of Cindy, the chaplain, and the coffin. He walked directly to the soldier.

"Corporal," the commander said, softly but firmly, "this is a private viewing. You will leave immediately." The soldier stayed at attention. The chaplain walked in with Cindy on his arm. She looked over at the soldier.

"Roy!" she called. The chaplain and commander turned to her. "Roy," she called out again, staring at the soldier, tears streaking her face.

The soldier stepped past the commander and walked directly to the sobbing woman. He kept his back to the officers, putting his hands on Cindy's shoulders and pulling her to him. She cried hysterically into his chest.

Though taken aback, Donner once again announced, "Soldier, this is private."

"Roy, what … what is going on?" Cindy said in a whisper. The soldier again put his hands on her shoulders, pushed her back a little, shook his head, and vanished.

Cindy put her face in her hands and sobbed. Donner, caught in midstride, looked around the small room for the soldier, finally staring at the chaplain.

"My God," the chaplain exclaimed, walking over to Cindy. He held her close and allowed himself to cry.

EIGHT

Dave Williams had not opened the tavern since the day his brother appeared. He needed time to sort things out. There had to be a mistake. Through the years he'd heard stories about how the service messed up when someone was killed. Sometimes there wasn't much left with which to make an identification, and he thought that might be the explanation. Maybe Joe was MIA, not KIA. The body identified as his brother's was someone else. Besides, how could he and his mother both see Joe alive and even embrace him if Joe was dead? Still, he could not understand where his brother had gone. One moment he was standing in the bar looking at him, and the next—poof.

Many times Dave tried calling the cell phone that he'd used to talk to Joe in the past, but the calls were never completed. Of course, he told himself, that didn't mean anything; cell phones in a war zone probably had a life expectancy of minutes. A call not getting connected now did not prove anything.

Jim Wilson, who had also seen Joe, didn't know what to say or do. He'd tried passing it off by saying Joe might be just having some fun, playing a joke. But when Joe didn't come back, he had nothing to say. He even had difficulty looking Dave directly in the eye for fear that Dave might see his own emotion. Every time he thought about the disappearance in connection with the phone call, it made the hair stand on the back of his neck.

The Defense Department had told Dave his brother's body would arrive that afternoon in Arizona and then flown to Seattle the next day. Dave was still more than a little doubtful that his brother's body would be in that coffin. He wanted to believe this was an understandable but unbelievably hurtful wartime screw up.

He sat with his wife, Lois, in their apartment. They had hardly spoken of anything other than of Joe's visit to the bar since the DOD notification to his mother and her call to him. Every time they tried, something about the bar would come up and Dave would think of Joe and become quiet, staring into space. Lois could see her husband reliving the experience each time.

The phone rang. Neither of them wanted to pick it up. After about ten rings, Dave finally reached for it.

"Hello" he said, almost in a whisper.

"Mr. Williams?" It was a woman's voice.

"Yes, who is this?"

"My name is Cindy Johnson, Mr. Williams. Your brother and my husband served together and were killed in battle the same night."

"Your husband was Roy Johnson?"

"Yes."

"Joe often talked of Roy. He was Joe's best friend in the service. I am so sorry for your loss, Mrs. Johnson. But I am not entirely convinced Joe is gone."

Cindy began to explain what happened to her, how Roy had arrived just moments before the two soldiers delivered the killed in action notification, how she ran through the house trying to find him, and what happened to Roy's parents just before she called them to tell them the news. Dave listened quietly, politely; Lois watched him intently. He did not respond when Cindy finished.

"Mr. Williams?" "Yes."

"There's more."

Cindy then explained what happened earlier that day at the airfield, how Roy was there again and how he shook his head, indicating she should not look in the coffin, and how the chaplain and the base commander both saw Roy.

"Mrs. Johnson," Dave said, "I really appreciate your call, and I'm not sure what to tell you about your husband. It all sounds very familiar, almost like what happened to me. But, unlike you, I'm still not sure Joe is dead. I will open the coffin tomorrow to see him to take away any doubts."

"Mr. Williams, I do so understand your feelings. I've come to accept that Roy was killed in action. But—"

"Could you wait one moment, Mrs. Johnson?" Dave interrupted. "Someone's at the door."

Lois got up, walked to the front door and looked through the view hole in the door. No one was there. Opening the door to double check, she said, "No one there, David—" She stopped in midsentence, frozen, her mouth still open to speak. In front of her, in full dress uniform, stood

Joe Williams. Joe was staring at his brother and shaking his head. The phone dropped to the floor.

Dave and Lois watched Joe for what seemed like minutes. He was healthy and clear eyed, looking first David, then at Lois, slowly shaking his head. Without warning, he just disappeared.

"Mr. Williams!" Cindy was still on the phone. "Mr. Williams!"

Dave reached down and picked up the phone. "Mrs. Johnson, I don't think it will be necessary for me to look in the coffin after all. My brother, Joe, was killed in action. I know it now without a doubt." He related to her what he'd just experienced.

"Mr. Williams—" Cindy started to talk again.

"I think you should call me Dave," he interrupted.

"Okay, if you'll call me Cindy. "They were killed in battle; that is obvious. But they are not gone. They're still with us."

Dave agreed, and took down her number and address. They exchanged condolences and a promise to keep in touch.

NINE

It was late in Germany. Nancy Savard slept earlier in the evening; she wanted to be as fresh as possible when she talked to Lance Kirkland, whom she remembered as being a scrupulous man, even if he did believe that armies of any type— military or spiritual—served a greater purpose. They'd had a most heated debate on the "higher purpose" of war. Knowing that they had such different views, she was confused about why she felt it necessary to contact him. Wouldn't he have an opposite view on what she was hearing and researching? Maybe she needed that opposite view to keep her in check.

She waited until six p.m. Arizona time to dial. There was no answer. Disappointed, she decided to go to bed. At least she could get a couple more of hours of sleep and then call him later in the day to make alternate arrangements. She'd no more than closed her eyes when the phone rang. It was Lance Kirkland.

"I just tried to call you," she said.

"I know. I was not in a good place to talk," he explained, "and it took me a little while to find a place."

"Understandable."

"So, I'm surprised you are still in the service to our country," Kirkland declared. "I thought by now you would be out of the evil military and working in private practice."

Nancy took a loud deep breath. "The military still gives me the greatest range of patients for research. A private hospital in the States would have me on one floor, constantly dealing with the same health issues over and over again. And, almost none of those cases would have the psychological implications I see here."

"So you now like war?" Kirkland asked with a twinge of sarcasm.

"No, I leave that in your hands, Chaplain," she said, mimicking his tone. "Lance," she continued after a short pause, "I need to talk to you about something other than our opposing views on war."

"What's up?"

Nancy started to tell Kirkland about her latest assignment in the U.S. military hospital in Germany, explaining in detail the severity of the wounds and that they were accompanied by unusual psychological phenomena.

"What type of psychological phenomena?"

"I have a sergeant here, Gabriel Gordon," she told him. "He was lucky to have kept his legs. Due to his injuries and the severe loss of blood, he saw unexplainable things during the two weeks he was in a coma."

She went on to explain how the two men in his unit protected him on the battlefield, then were killed by friendly fire. She told him how he "saw" the two men, after he knew they were dead, go to their homes in the U.S. and visit their loved ones just before the Department of Defense delivered the news. She explained in detail what he "saw" about Cindy Johnson.

Kirkland was silent with disbelief.

"Lance? Are you still there?" She looked at the phone, wondering if they'd been disconnected.

It was a few more seconds before Kirkland answered. "Nancy, I'm sorry. At first I thought you were telling me old ghost stories that have been around and around. Are you at liberty to tell me the name of the servicemen who were killed?"

"I shouldn't."

"Can you confirm?" His question surprised her.

"Okay, I can do that."

"Corporal Roy Johnson?"

Nancy felt the hair on the back of her neck stand on end.

He explained his experience with Cindy Johnson, how she was determined that the Defense Department had it wrong because she'd held Roy in her arms. He went through the whole story.

"That sounds like what Gabriel reported," Nancy said.

Kirkland then told her what had happened at the hangar earlier that afternoon, including the fact that everyone present, including the base commander, had seen Roy Johnson hold his wife and let her know no other proof was needed.

It was Nancy's turn to be quiet.

"Nancy?"

"Lance, there's something else. While Sergeant Gordon was in a coma, two soldiers in full dress would stand at the foot of his bed each night, every night for two weeks. Others in the ward saw them, too."

"Only at night?"

"That's what they tell me. They appeared as soon as the ward lights were turned off."

Now they both were quiet.

"Why are you assigned to that ward?"

"I'm not sure that's the right question. I'm not assigned; it is a choice. All the men in this ward have similar tales to tell, including one who saw the visit of a dead enemy soldier before his family received his remains."

She shared that story, too, ending with, "The American soldier telling the tale reported it as if he was there."

"So the Army is keeping these men together?"

"Unofficially, it seems," she told him. "I can't find anything that shows any specific reason for these men to be kept together. They didn't serve in the same unit or the same area. However, they are the most severely wounded in the hospital."

"Well, it could be the severity of their wounds, I suppose. But, tell me, what do you think?"

"Well, I honestly don't know what to think. But that is also one of the reasons why I am calling you."

"Hmm," Kirkland said, allowing a bit of sarcasm back into the conversation. "You're calling a pro-war chaplain halfway around the world, asking him for a reason why these men are being kept together?"

"Sort of," she responded. "You got a gut feeling?"

"I think there's a connection between these men but it might not be the ghost stories."

"These are *not* ghost stories," she insisted, feeling the same old polarizing stance taking hold.

"We obviously need a lot more information," Kirkland stated.

"I will be talking quite often with Sergeant Gordon," she told Kirkland, "and if anything interesting comes up, I'll give you a call."

TEN

Gabriel Gordon woke early and listened to the activity in the hall pick up as shifts changed and breakfast was being prepared. The stillness inside the ward began to fade as men woke.

Sergeant. Sergeant," Washington whispered. Gabriel looked at him. "Do you see them?"

"Who?"

"The soldiers."

"I've not seen any soldiers other than you," Gabriel said.

Washington nodded and lay back on his bed. Gabriel wondered, what soldiers? and then dozed back to sleep, only to be awakened by the sound of breakfast trays being brought into the ward by the orderlies. It was the usual: runny eggs, cereal, and coffee.

Gabriel gave a disinterested try at the cereal and coffee. He was surprised to see Nurse Savard tending to the lieutenant before she went to check the dressing Allan's dressing. Allan was awake but not in good spirits. Then she came over to Gabriel's bed.

"Good morning, Gabe," she said too cheerfully. She looked tired.

"Morning," he said. "You up late?"

"Nah, up early. Not hungry?"

"Not into runny eggs."

"You should try to eat them anyway."

"Here, you eat them." He handed her the metal tray.

"I've already eaten," she joked, "and I'm watching my figure."

"Me, too," he said with a smile.

"You should eat," she teased. "Those eggs could only help *your* figure."

Gabriel looked down the ward and did not see the soldier he'd spoken with earlier.

"Where is he?" Gabriel asked, looking at the bare mattress on the bed Washington occupied.

"Who? Washington?"

"I was just talking with him earlier little while ago. Where did he go?"

Nancy looked at him questioningly. "You talked to him?

"Yeah. He asked if I saw the soldiers."

"When was this?"

"Before six, five fifteen, five thirty, maybe."

"Sergeant, are you sure about that time?"

"Give or take, yeah."

"Private Washington passed around eleven. last night," Nancy said softly.

"No, that can't be. He was talking to me this morning. When I told him I didn't see the soldiers, he just lay down," Gabriel explained, as he looked at Lieutenant Stiles who had arrived and was sitting at the edge of his bed.

"They wheeled him out of here around midnight, Sergeant," Dan told him.

"I'll be back in a little while for some rehab work," Nurse Savard said. "Maybe I'll get you out for a bit today to get some fresh air."

Gabriel stared at the empty bed.

"And try to eat these eggs," she said.

Allan tapped on the tray to get Gabriel's attention. "This type of shit happens all the time around here," he said.

"How long you been here?"

"Four months. I was very badly burned and kept sedated for the first two. So, when I came around, I thought all the people I'd been seeing were from the drugs, especially when they told me that there had been no one in to see me," Allan explained. "But I still saw them, long after the drugs were stopped."

"Saw who?"

"Mostly soldiers, but occasionally sailors, Marines, even Air Force. They're always full dress, always quiet. They take turns standing watch at the foot of someone's bed."

"Did you see them at Washington's?"

"Every day until yesterday. Nothing yesterday," Allan said. "I thought I was healing more and some of these visions were wearing off. But Washington was like the others."

"What others?"

"The others who die here. The day before they die, soldiers don't stand at their beds.

It seems—or at least what I make of it is—that theses soldiers no longer need to stand watch on someone who's going to pass, ready to pass."

"Are you sure you're seeing soldiers?"

"Are you sure you saw Washington this morning?" Allan answered flatly.

The lieutenant still sat on the bed, listening to the conversation.

"Do you still see soldiers around me?" Gabriel wanted to know.

"The same two as before. But they're more relaxed with you than when you first came in. They aren't really standing at attention. They're here and watching you, but seem to be less concerned."

"Parade rest?"

"Yeah, that might be it. Hands behind their backs, legs spread apart, though they will look around and at each other, which was something they didn't do while you were unconscious."

Gabriel pointed to the lieutenant and shrugged.

"Mine are still here, Sergeant," Dan called out. Allan nodded.

Gabriel thought about Washington, how he'd talked with the man that morning. But both the nurse and the lieutenant confirmed that he'd passed the night before, and now his bed was stripped and empty. Allan said it was a pattern. Gabriel was confused.

What is going on? Why did I dream of Johnson and Williams with their families until the DOD arrived, and why did my father say Johnson and Williams stayed with him and Mom until the "all clear" was given on my surgery?

An orderly entered the ward and stopped at Gabriel's bed, looking at the uneaten eggs.

"You hungry?" Gabriel asked.

While the orderly was cleaning up, Nancy arrived, followed by a nurse carrying bags of gauze and cotton. Nancy smiled at Gabriel as she and the other nurse walked to Allan's bed. "We'll be gentle, Corporal. But, like before, some of these bandages may pull at the burned areas as we remove them."

"This ain't my first rodeo," Allan remarked. Everyone laughed, including Gabriel and the lieutenant.

The ward did seem brighter today. The sunlight coming in the windows gave a cheerful feel to the drab colored facility. Gabriel tried to keep his eyes from Allan's bed, hoping to give the corporal some sense of privacy, but the activity of the two nurses kept catching his attention. Each time he looked over, he quickly turned in another direction.

Allan attempted to smile, but many times with the attempt turned into a grimace. When his bandages were finally replaced, he seemed more comfortable. There were noticeably fewer now, allowing more of his face to be seen. He still had his head wrapped, but his face remained clear except for a bandage on his right cheek.

"This feels much better," he said. The nurse cleaned up and took away the old bandages while Nancy approached Gabriel.

"We need to tend to the lieutenant," she told him. "Then we'll get your legs moving."

"I can hardly wait," Gabriel said.

"Sergeant," Allan whispered, "Washington's soldiers were by his bed this morning even though he was already gone."

"They came back to an empty bed?"

"First time I've seen them do that," Allan admitted.

"Are they there now?"

"I never see them in the daylight."

Gabriel was leaning toward the corporal's bed, straining to hear every word. "Why are you talking so quietly?"

Allan's eyes moved slightly, looking over the sergeant's shoulder.

"Another union meeting?" Nancy asked.

"We are caucusing on who the union's president will be," Gabriel joked back.

"Who's running?"

"Just you," Gabriel said. "We thought brains and beauty would be tough to beat."

"Sergeant, you must be feeling better." She smiled. Gabriel didn't smile back.

"How about getting out of here?" she proposed.

"Sure, what do you have in mind? Dinner and dancing?"

"Maybe next time," she told him. An orderly steered a worn looking wheelchair over to the bed. The leather seat and back did not look comfortable.

"It rides better than it looks," the orderly promised.

Nancy and the orderly positioned the chair so that Gabriel could get into it with as little effort as possible. She held him by the left arm and then instructed the orderly to hold the other; they lifted.

"Sergeant," Nancy grunted, "it is okay to help." Gabriel put a little weight on his legs as he tried to lift himself off the bed.

"Ahhh," he said. "I can feel my legs." He slipped back.

"Well, we don't have to do this today," Nancy said.

He tried once more and this time succeeded in getting himself to the edge of the bed. The orderly wheeled over the frame and positioned it so that he could grab the handle.

"Pull yourself up and we'll get the chair under you," Nancy instructed.

While standing, Gabriel tested the strength in his legs by easing off on how much weight his arms were holding. He grimaced almost immediately.

"I bet that hurt," Nancy said.

"Just a bit," he admitted.

"Well, it's encouraging that you're feeling stronger, but you need to be careful. Too much too soon can be dangerous," she warned.

After the chair was under him, Nancy and the orderly positioned themselves on each arm, helping Gabriel lower himself.

"So," Nancy said, "that went well."

"Just like we learned in boot camp," Gabriel said.

ELEVEN

Outside of the ward there was more activity but nothing directly in front of the ward's door. The nurse's station, a few steps to the left, was bustling with busy nurses, orderlies, and some doctors. Some were in military dress and others wore hospital uniforms. After all this time, Gabriel thought the sight of military uniforms looked out of place.

"I'm still in the Army!" he joked.

The activity diminished the further from the station they went, giving the hall a deserted feeling. Nancy walked ahead and ran a card through a reader on the wall, opening two double doors toward them and revealing a long gray hallway on the other side.

"I'll take it from here," she told the orderly, pushing the chair through the door. The hallway's chill matched its gray color.

"Forget to pay the heating bill?" Gabriel teased.

"The only areas in this section that are lit and heated in the winter or cooled in the summer are the offices. The hallways do not get anything except maybe emergency lighting," Nancy told him.

"Offices?" Gabriel was surprised. "I thought we were going for some kind of rehab exercises.

"We are."

Nancy pushed him down the hallway. Once they passed a slight curve, Gabriel saw some light through windows set in doors along the corridor. They walked down to the end and turned right.

"My office is up on the left," Nancy said.

"Wow, they give nurses their own office. I knew I entered the wrong part of the Army."

She stopped on the left in front of another two doors, sliding her card through the reader and, opening the doors to her office, pushing Gabriel inside. The light caused him to squint at first but he adjusted quickly.

"Are these real plants and flowers?" They covered the large office on one side near the windows, some blooming and running from the floor to the ceiling and the full length of the front wall.

"Surprised?"

"I haven't seen anything blooming since I left home. They don't seem real." "This room," she said, "was meant to be a solarium. When I first got here, it was empty, so I asked for it. Seemed the budget included a solarium to be built but not maintained."

"So how does a nurse get the penthouse suite? I would think that a doctor—maybe the Surgeon General—would get an office like this."

"I am a doctor."

"But you do nurse-type duties and even wear a nurse's uniform."

Nancy took some time to explain that, after she received her doctorate, she also received her nursing degree.

"Why would a psychiatrist want a nursing degree?"

She pushed him over to the plants and squatted in front of him, eye to eye. "I thought that, in order to help people heal mentally, I should be able to work with them on a physical level."

Gabriel said nothing; he shifted a little in the wheelchair.

"It has worked well. I've learned a lot about helping people psychologically through their physical healing and needs."

"Why did you wheel me all the way here?" Gabriel asked. "To smell the roses?"

"Sergeant," she started to speak.

"Ah, now the rank comes in. Up until now it's mostly been 'Gabe.'"

"Well, Gabe," Nancy said, sounding a bit more relaxed, "if that's what you prefer, a change in scenery always helps in recovery. And, you're right; first names help in communications."

"So I should call you?"

"Nancy is fine with me."

Gabriel nodded and added "Me, too. So, we work my legs where?"

"Back in the ward."

"This is where we work on my mind?"

"This is where we work on other things."

"Like?"

"You've been through extreme trauma, with serious wounds to your legs. And emotional trauma by watching your men, who were trying to save you, get killed by friendly fire. Plus, remaining unconscious for two weeks poses serious trauma to your mind."

"Great!" Gabriel responded quickly.

"What about Washington?"

"He passed during the night; you told me so yourself."

"Yes, I did."

"The kid seemed okay yesterday."

"He shouldn't have made it as long as he did," Nancy noted. "But you told me you talked to him this morning."

"I must have been asleep, dreaming I was awake."

"What about the other dreaming? Let's talk about Williams."

"Not much to say," Gabriel responded. He did not look at her eyes. "Good soldier; cared about what he was doing."

"You saw him get shot," she said.

"Yeah, he and Johnson were trying to get the attention of a truck for me." Gabriel's voice trailed off. Nancy stopped for a moment to study his reaction. "He made too much noise trying to get some extra ammo and caught the attention of others across the field," Gabriel said.

"Gabriel," Nancy spoke slower, "didn't you see Joe in his brother's bar in Seattle?"

"Probably a dream."

"Care to explain the dream?"

"Not really."

"Well, we can spend some time talking about the flowers — maybe two or three hours."

"But I explained this all to you once"

"Yes, but we were in the ward with a lot of other people around."

"Joe's brother was opening the bar in the middle of the afternoon. Someone, I guess one of the regular patrons, was waiting for him. As he was opening the door and letting the patron in, he saw a soldier walking down the street." He recounted all he could remember of the "dream".

"What do you think of that dream?" she asked.

"I think that is a question for you, Doc," Gabriel said. After a few moments, he continued, "I don't know. Maybe I feel guilty about him dying to save my life and I didn't want anyone to be hurt. So I made up the scenario in my head: his brother gets to see Joe one more time."

"Not bad," Nancy said. "What about Johnson?"

"Oh, come on. It was pretty much the same dream. Johnson shows up at his door moments before his wife gets the news and then she can't find him. Same issue with dreaming about Johnson's parents."

"Seems logical," she said. "So how do you explain your parents dreaming that people named Johnson and Williams were sitting with them while you were in surgery?"

"I can't explain other people's dreams; I have enough on my hands with my own," Gabriel exclaimed.

Nancy waited.

"Okay, here's a shot." Gabriel raised his arms. "Johnson and Williams were looking out for me while I was hurt. I am transferring my worry for them to worry about my family."

"And your parents picked up on that from what? Christmas cards?"

"I told you it was a shot."

"Good."

"So I'm fit for duty?"

"Yep, but let's talk a bit."

Nancy gave a brief explanation about a plane that landed at a military base carrying the bodies of servicemen killed in action.

"Are you trying to help me put this thing to rest with a story about the dead flying home?"

"Yep." She told him about the wife of a slain serviceman who wanted to see the body of her husband so she could come to terms with the fact that he had actually been killed in battle. Included in her explanation was how the coffin was being moved across a large deserted hangar and a soldier was waiting in an empty room on the other side.

"When the coffin was wheeled into the room, the wife recognized the soldier as her husband. He held her and shook his head no, then disappeared. Since she no longer needed proof, she did not open the coffin. There were two other officers with her: the chaplain and the base commander. They both saw the soldier."

"This actually happened?" Gabriel asked.

Nancy nodded. "To Cindy Johnson, the wife of Corporal Roy Johnson."

Gabriel's face lost all color. Raising his right arm, he rubbed the back of his neck.

"How do you know this?"

"I know the chaplain."

"Are you telling me I was not dreaming?"

"Maybe, but your dreams related to what actually happened," she said.

"To Joe Williams?"

"And your parents," she said, standing up behind the wheelchair.

"You're going to drop that on me and then wheel me back?"

"We are just starting," she said and wheeled him over to the other side of the large room, which resembled more of an office, with waiting room-type couches, chairs, and bookcases lining the walls.

"You are in a ward with others who have experienced similar visions," she explained.

"Visions? So you're not calling them dreams?"

"If you don't like the word 'visions,' we can use something else. But I believe they are more than dreams."

"Visions. I guess I'll get used to that. Are they caused by the trauma?"

"I don't know," she responded. "But my feeling is that since you're seeing what others are experiencing, there's more than trauma involved. Even though you all are not seeing the same things, the scenarios are so similar that there has to be a connection, even with someone seeing the enemy."

"The lieutenant?"

"For one."

"So it seems we're all in that ward for the same reason," Gabriel said. "But I was unconscious for two weeks; how did you know to put me in there?"

"Besides what you were saying in your dreams? Maybe just by chance," she said. "When you came in, Dr. Sierra, who worked on you in the war zone, was working with Allan and it was just a matter of convenience to have you close by. It wasn't until you woke up that we realized you were in the right place."

"The right place for treatment?"

"We are not looking ... I should say, *I* am not looking to cure you of what you're seeing. I want to find out why you are seeing it," Nancy stated.

"You mean what causes it?"

"Not so much the nuts and bolts, but, rather, why certain individuals in certain situations."

"So this doesn't happen to everyone?"

Nancy thought for a moment before responding. "No, it does not seem to happen to everyone. But it does seem to happen in every war."

"So every war has these 'ghost stories?'"

"There are always stories about how when soldiers, or even civilians, pass, they somehow deliver a message or an indication—a shadow, a thought— to a loved one," Nancy said. "But, in certain wars, especially more recent wars, these stories have become more involved, with more people seeing the dead. There seems to be a larger thought going on, and there is a physical presence of the deceased."

"It doesn't make sense."

"No, it does not. And we don't know what, or even if, something is going on."

"So we're being studied," Gabriel said.

"Well, I'm not even sure if there is an 'official' reason why you're being kept together. And as far as I'm concerned, I really don't know what questions to ask you. So studies, if you want to call them that, are more than limited. Maybe we can find similarities in personalities, relationships, or backgrounds. We really don't even know where to start."

"So what's next?"

"I don't know," she admitted. "I have asked the chaplain I just told you about to come here."

"Why?"

"He would have some reasoning from a different point of view than mine."

"You mean, being a chaplain, he would be more in tune spiritually?"

"That could be part of it."

"What else?"

"He's been involved with more wars than I, so he has more experience dealing with emotional trauma and death." She purposefully left out out the pro-war stance that the chaplain hung on to.

"How long have these studies been going on?"

"You trying to trap me, Gabe? There are no official studies. I'm interested, and I hope I can help you."

"Well, are there written records of other soldiers and other wars involving these experiences?"

"No one is studying this or comparing war to war." Nancy had an odd look on her face, as if she was trying to convey something other than what she was saying.

"I'm confused," Gabriel said.

"We all are," Nancy responded. "We should be getting you back."

"Nice flowers," he commented.

They rolled past the nurse's station and then into the ward. "You survived and back in one piece?" the lieutenant asked.

An orderly helped Nancy get Gabe back into his bed. She then placed a hand under his ankle the other under his calf and lifted both legs a few times. Then she propped up his pillows. "Remember, don't take anything unless I tell you it's okay," she whispered in his ear.

"Why?" he asked as she walked away.

"Where did they take you?" Allan wanted to know.

"Out for a spin. Just a change in scenery," Gabriel said, uncertain of how much to share

"Did you see the flowers?"

Gabriel nodded.

TWELVE

Lance Kirkland was in the commander's office waiting. Donner had called the night before, wanting to discuss what they'd seen at the hangar. Lance knew he didn't have any answers. *Two military men discussing a ghost?* It didn't seem like a normal discussion between officers, even if one of them was a chaplain.

"Chaplain." Donner nodded as he walked in.

"Good morning, Sir." Kirkland stood.

"No need for that, Lance," Donner said, sitting down. "This discussion goes above and beyond, so to speak." He feel silent, trying to find the right words to begin. Finally, he said, "What did we see, Lance?"

The chaplain shifted in his seat. "We saw many things: a solemn ceremony in which war dead were returned home; the bravery of a slain soldier's wife needing confirmation; and a soldier giving her that confirmation."

"You call it confirmation?" Donner asked, surprised.

"On the surface."

"What else?"

The chaplain once again shifted in his seat. He turned his head and looked out the window across the airfield, then stood up and walked to that window. "Let's start with the wildest and work backward," he proposed.

"We saw a ghost, the spirit of a fallen soldier," Donner announced.

"A ghost. Okay, why?"

"A guess here," Donner said, "but there are theories that people who pass contact loved ones to get a final message to them, a way of saying goodbye or showing comfort."

"Maybe."

"Lance, you spoke with Cindy Johnson in order to arrange this viewing. You told me that Corporal Johnson was at her home before the two officers arrived with the news that Johnson was KIA. If that was the case, wouldn't the theory for that visit be the final message?"

"That is the way I'd interpret it," Kirkland responded.

"Then what did we see?"

"We may have been experiencing a certain amount of group

hypnosis, sympathy for what the woman was about to go through. We all knew the story, so we conjured this apparition—or what we've interpreted to be an apparition."

"I was empathetic to her. I considered what she requested to be wrong and very painful. If it wasn't for your recommendation, I would have never approved it," Donner stated.

"So you did not see the soldier?"

"Jesus, Lance. I saw the damned soldier. I saw him standing in the room from across the hangar. I saw him hold Mrs. Johnson and then shake his head. That was not imagination or a sympathetic reaction. I know what I saw."

"He disappeared," Dan said flatly.

"I saw him disappear, and I also saw Cindy Johnson accept the fact that her husband's body was in the coffin."

"Then, sir, we all saw a ghost."

"I can't disagree, but we will keep this as quiet as we can while trying to find some answers. Are there others who have experienced what we have?"

"I think so."

They discussed his call from Nancy Savard the night before. He included their history, their opposite views on war and the military, and then explained the research she was doing in that ward in Germany.

"So, she is doing a study on this?" the commander asked.

"Yes. Though I think it's unofficial."

"How do we get more information?"

"She asked me to come there."

"So you would fly to Germany and get involved?"

"Involved … well, like I said, her research is not officially official. I'm not sure who knows of it besides her and what she told me in a private conversation."

"Well, I will come up with something that will get you there for an official matter, and it will be up to you how and when to work with her."

"Fine. When do I leave?"

The commander picked up the phone and asked for the flight schedule. After waiting on hold for a few seconds, he made an acknowledgement and said to the chaplain, "There is a flight out tonight."

"I'll be on it."

THIRTEEN

Three helicopters set out on a reconnaissance mission over the water just off the beach, flying in formation, with the lead chopper slightly lower than the other two. Since they were trying to locate enemy positions that could observe ship movements off the coast, the side doors closest to the beach were open.

Airman Cliff Craft, flying in the third helicopter, scanned the shoreline though large black binoculars. "Not seeing much," he said.

"You got the lens caps off there, Craft?" asked the pilot, Steve McCafferty, through his headset.

"No, sir. I thought that would be the best way to avoid a fight."

The pilot laughed.

"Most of this place has been blown apart; doesn't seem to be much left to hide behind," Craft continued.

McCafferty looked to his left, seeing the same war-torn beach that Craft was scanning. "I must have flown over this beach a dozen times in the last week; haven't seen as much as a rat."

"Who makes the decision on what to recon?" James Hewson, the gunner, asked.

"Someone in the head, back at HQ. Depends on what direction the pointy ends of their turds indicate," Craft replied.

The lead chopper lifted a little, and McCafferty saw a trail of smoke coming from the beach a few hundred yards ahead of them. A low thud rumbled inside McCafferty's chopper as he witnessed the lead helicopter's bottom blow out. Pieces of the seats and a stilled body fell to the water, and the chopper started to spiral. As the props slowed, the body of the aircraft started spinning in the opposite direction.

McCafferty slowed his chopper and maneuvered up. As he did, he could see inside the falling helicopter as it slowly rotated, and watched the pilot slapping at the flames on his chest.

"No, Danny, no," McCafferty screamed in desperation. Danny Mellon, whom he had known since they were in flight school, was being burned to death before his eyes.

The third helicopter went low and took a track on the area where the RPG had been from. The lead chopper continued to rotate down toward the water. Each spin showed more and more of the panic the pilot was going through, looking more like slow motion and special effects from movie than an actual live event. After the fourth rotation, the pilot no longer slapped at his chest. He was leaning back against his seat with red and yellow flames up to and surrounding his head.

Then, oddly, everything was momentarily quiet until the chopper hit the water and exploded long heartbeats later, sending a huge yellow flash and pieces of blades high into the sky. A broken blade headed toward McCafferty's chopper, spinning end over end.

"Get us out of here," Hewson screamed.

The blade, as if directed by radio signal, positioned itself perfectly, flattening out and entering the pilot's side of the chopper. It took off the top of McCafferty's helmet, leaving the sides to catch the blood and brains that spilled out of the pilot's head. The blade did not stop but continued back to Craft, impaling him in the chest.

"No, Chris," Hewson cried out, reaching for Craft, who died instantly.

The chopper turned on its right side and started going down. Hewson climbed past Craft and jumped out, hitting the water at the same time as the falling chopper. He surfaced and tried swimming away, but found he could not move his left arm. So he used his right arm to side paddle his way a safe distance. As he swam, the water became shallower and he was able to pull himself toward the beach by digging into the rough sand with the fingertips of his right hand.

The third chopper had done its job clearing the area where the rocket came from and circled overhead, staying as close to Hewson as possible. He tried waving the okay to the chopper but, each time he raised his right arm, his head went underwater. The world was getting gray and less detailed and, at one point, he thought he saw someone jump out of the circling chopper. A few seconds later, someone put his arms around Hewson's chest and pulled him the rest of the way onto the beach. He noticed the color of the shore near him turning red.

"Don't worry, Gunny, we got medics coming." The soldier who jumped out of the chopper was working on his left arm and assuring him he would be taken care of.

Hewson heard more choppers coming in, seeing a familiar red cross out of the corner of his eye as he lay on the beach in water only an inch deep. Two more soldiers wearing wetsuits came up from the water and took over working on his left arm. A chopper positioned itself directly overhead. Again, Hewson saw the two familiar intersecting red lines on its underbelly and watched as a basket was lowered. He felt very light, and saw the metal edges of the basket from the corner of his eyes. He lay still for a moment and then felt himself being lifted.

The basket spun slowly and, as he turned, he looked up the beach to the area that the first chopper had cleared; it was still on fire. Four bodies were lined up, one blackened and three still burning. Beside each body, someone stood, looked at the bodies, and then at Hewson. McCafferty and Craft were in the chopper, smiling and nodding at him, as he was pulled in. The buttons and medals from their full dress uniforms shone in Hewson's eyes; their faces were bright, as if a white light was on them. Behind McCafferty and Craft, there were other men, also nodding, in uniforms he didn't recognize. One saluted.

Hewson blinked his eyes.

"I'm a medic," he was told. "We're getting you to a surgical hospital." Hewson heard himself moan with pain.

The medic reached into a box, pulled out a small packet, broke it and stuck something into Hewson's left shoulder, bringing tears to his eyes. Hewson saw the same four men who were on the beach and recognized the enemy dress uniform. They nodded at him and, again, one saluted. He closed his eyes.

When he opened his eyes again, his surroundings had changed. There was a man with a white surgical mask standing over him.

"We are going to help you, soldier; do your best to help us," came the voice from behind the mask.

***

Hewson followed McCafferty as they walked down a long country road. McCafferty was still in the full dress uniform he'd worn on the Red Cross chopper and was walking as though marching: back straight, hands at his side, fingers together, palms facing in. Hewson had on what he'd worn in the water, his left side still covered with blood, though he realized he was able to move his left arm. He had trouble keeping up with McCafferty; no matter how hard he tried, he could not catch up with the pilot.

He tried calling out to McCafferty but made no sound, his mouth only forming the words. McCafferty turned his head and nodded but kept marching, never varying his speed, always keeping the same distance between them. It was springtime here, with the sun shining through the blossoming trees, and birds and squirrels easily moving from branch to branch as if following the same rhythm McCafferty was marching to.

The pilot came to a long dirt driveway that led to a large log home tucked back behind some trees. There was an old Ford pickup in the driveway and a much newer model sedan sitting next to it. Making an official tight military turn, McCafferty walked up the driveway. Hewson followed.

An older man sat on the porch. Hewson guessed he was in his mid-seventies. When the old man noticed them walking up the driveway, he stood slowly, squinting, and walked to the porch steps, never taking his eyes off the approaching soldier, even as he hobbled down the steps to meet him.

McCafferty came to a stop a few feet in front of the old man, clicked his heels and saluted. The old man laughed. Or, rather, his mouth moved but nothing came out, causing Hewson to poke at his ears as if trying to clear them. The old man's mouth moved again, then he reached out and took Steve's hand, reaching behind the pilot with his other arm pulling him close. McCafferty matched the old man's hug, pulling him tight. A tear ran down the old man's face.

The sound of a vehicle came from the dirt road. Hewson slapped at the side of his head to confirm that his ears were actually starting to work. He turned to see the familiar green official vehicle stopping by the mailbox at the end of the driveway before coming up the driveway. The old man broke his hold on McCafferty and walked toward the approaching vehicle.

Two officers stepped out and greeted the old man. They spoke for a moment, but Hewson was too far away to hear the conversation. The old man looked surprised, then he smiled and shook his head. He started turning and saying something over his shoulder to the officers while pointing at the house, then stopped abruptly. His visitor had vanished.

The old man left the two soldiers, saying something as he walked away up the steps and into the house. The two soldiers could see the old man t going from room to room. He stepped out on the front porch, with his mouth forming the word "Steve."

The officers approached and spoke with the old man, who now looked much older and visibly shaken. A sound came to Hewson, the sound of an old man's broken heart. The officers reached out, taking the older man by the arms and helping him sit. Every few seconds, Hewson saw the old man's mouth shape the name "Steve." But Steve McCafferty was gone.

***

Hewson found himself on a bus going up a long winding mountain road. It was a clear day with bright sunshine and blue sky. In the distance, a large lake and white covered distant mountains filled the frame of his left side window.

Children ran up and down the aisle of the bus despite many objections from the driver, who finally picked up a microphone and asked the parents to control them. A heavyset, brown haired woman in a white shirt and stretch pants got up from the rear and took one of the children, a boy, back with her. She said something to the child that made him laugh. He laughed so hard it made Hewson laugh, and the bus driver, looking at them via the rearview mirror, started laughing also. The boy sat happily with a book on his lap, occasionally saying something while the woman watched contentedly.

The bus continued up the road. The views were spectacular. The road wound around sharp, narrow curves, causing the passengers to jokingly voice their concerns whenever they were forced to lean one way or another.

The bus pulled off to the right. An elderly woman with perfectly combed white hair stood and slowly walked up the aisle, then waited patiently until the driver got out of his seat to help her down the steps. They stood outside the door talking for a few moments; it was obvious they knew each other. The driver took the woman's hand in his and patted it, then climbed back up on the bus. The bus took off, slowly gaining speed up a long incline.

Hewson noticed a woman sitting directly across from him. She seemed anxious, biting her lower lip. At each turn, she would look ahead and then at her watch.

The bus slowed as it approached what appeared to be another stop. A soldier in full dress uniform stood by the stop that was covered by a short wooden roof. Hewson didn't know if he knew the soldier, as his view was obstructed by the other passengers. The woman across from him also noticed the soldier. She seemed surprised, at first, but then a look of fear and dread spread across her face. She turned away, forcing herself to look out the other side of the bus.

When the vehicle came to a full stop, the woman walked to the front with obvious reluctance. Hewson felt compelled to follow in an effort to identify the half seen soldier. It was Craft, standing straighter and showing more respect for the uniform then Hewson could ever remember. Cliff Craft, who he remembered seeing with a helicopter blade impaling him to the wall of a chopper, who he last saw standing, in the same full dress uniform, on the Red Cross chopper.

The woman stepped down from the bus, not answering the driver's goodbye nor walking around to the other side where the soldier was. Instead, she kept her back to the bus as it pulled away, which also meant she had her back to Craft.

"Clifford," she whispered, breathing heavily, "I will not look at you." Her voice was weak and emotional. "You coming home without notice, especially in uniform, means you are not really here. I don't want to face it. I won't face it. I cannot say goodbye to my son," she whispered. "A mother should never have to face this moment."

Hewson felt a chill as the wind picked up.

"Clifford, I will not turn to look at you," she said, louder and more insistent.

She turned left and walked up the road, very slowly pulling her sweater up around her neck as the wind blew still harder, causing leaves and branches to slide across the pavement. Craft followed, matching her pace.

She walked for a couple of hundred yards, the wind now howling around her and pushing her up the road as she struggled with her balance. Craft kept the same distance behind, with Hewson trailing after. She walked across the road and up the driveway to a small white cottage. Craft continued to follow.

Hewson heard the sound of tires coming from the road. The vehicle wasn't traveling fast, just steady. Craft stood at the bottom of the steps. His mother turned, looking in the direction of the approaching car and positioned her shoulder to block the view of her son.

The vehicle slowed, stopped briefly, and turned in. She whimpered softly at the sight of the green government car. Crumpling the top step, she put her hands over her face. Craft sat and put his arms around her as she sobbed aloud. The wind stopped. She rested her head on her son's shoulder as both doors on the car opened and two grim faced soldiers exited and slowly approached.

FOURTEEN

Nurse Savard stood over James Hewson as he woke up. "Good afternoon, James," she said. He tried to answer but his mouth was too dry. She gave him some water, holding his head up and a straw to his lower lip. The water helped him move his lips and the tongue that seemed to be glued to them.

"How are you feeling?"

"Tired and sore," he said in a hoarse whisper.

"You are in the Army hospital in Germany. Do you know where that is?"

"I'd probably need directions," he said, his voice starting to clear.

"Sense of humor is a good sign." Nancy laughed. "So you must be feeling good enough to make jokes."

"Not really," he responded. He touched his left side with his right hand and felt a lot of bandages. Running his fingers down, he searched for his left hand.

"James." Nancy put her hands to his face, wanting him to look her in the eye. "You lost your left arm from just below your shoulder."

Hewson breathed in quickly and started to cough. She handed him the cup of water again. He sipped a few times and slowly stopped coughing.

"Why?" His voice again raspy.

"The doctor can give the details, but there wasn't much to save. Whatever hit you took most of it away."

"McCafferty and Craft?"

"You've been talking about them while you were sleeping. If they were the ones in the helicopter with you, they died."

"That's right," Hewson said, nodding as he remembered.

"So you were having some vivid dreams?"

"Dreams?"

"Yes, you were talking about an older man searching for McCafferty and a woman crying, not wanting to see Craft." "Oh, yeah," Hewson said, "those dreams."

"We'll talk about them later." She checked his bandages, smiled, and walked away.

An orderly came to his bed almost immediately. "Dinner," he announced. I'm sure you must be hungry." He pointed to the IVs. "Not much in those things to fill you up."

"Not really hungry," Hewson answered, but the order left the tray and told him to eat what he could. Hewson stared at the food; it looked like soup and oatmeal. He pushed the tray aside, moved his right hand to his left side, and closed his eyes.

Gabriel Gordon,in the bed next to him, cleared his throat, hoping to get Hewson's attention. After there was no response, Gabriel cleared it again.

"You got a cold?" Hewson said, staring at the ceiling.

"Gabriel Gordon," came the reply.

"James Hewson. Now that we're lifelong buddies, I'm really not much in the mood for conversation."

"Understood," Gabriel said. "But, James, they *will* want you to talk about McCafferty and Craft."

"Seems those dead soldiers have generated some interest," Hewson said.

"Among other dead soldiers," Gabriel said flatly.

Dr. Sierra and Nurse Savard stopped to check on the lieutenant, and then continued on to the back of the ward.

"Gabriel," Dr. Sierra said, "you appear to be recovering well."

"You'd be the judge of that," Gabriel responded. "However, I am feeling better."

The doctor checked the bandages and then walked over to Allan's bed, looking at the corporal's eyes and checking his bandages before turning to Hewson. Nancy was already there, looking at the uneaten dinner.

"Not hungry," Hewson explained.

"How are you feeling, James?" Dr. Sierra asked, clipboard in his hands, without looking at the soldier.

"Ready to do some pull ups or maybe play guitar," Hewson responded.

Dr. Sierra glanced at Nancy. "James," Dr. Sierra said, "your arm was very badly damaged by the helicopter that blew up in front of you; there was not much to save. The report I read said you pulled yourself through it all, including jumping from the falling helicopter and swimming away from the wreckage. It evens says you gave the surgeon some advice before you went under: 'You do your part and I'll do mine.'"

"Funny," Hewson noted. "I thought the surgeon said that to me."

"I know it is difficult and it will take a lot of getting used to but, with rehab, you should do fine."

"How does someone play the guitar with one arm?"

"I don't know, James, Dr. Sierra said with some care. "You just rest. We'll be close by." The doctor walked away.

"So you like music?" Nancy asked.

"Yep."

"You play?"

"Not anymore." Hewson looked her in the eyes.

"Ever try the piano?"

"When I was a kid."

"Good," Nancy said. "I know you can play the piano with one hand. I'll check to see what I can find out about the guitar."

She turned and left the ward. Hewson lifted his head to watch her as she walked away.

The ward was quiet except for the sound of metal trays being moved in the hallway. Dan Stiles moved over to the side of his bed, grabbed his crutches, and started down to the end of the ward.

"How's the newcomer?" Allan asked.

"That is what I'm going to find out," Dan said.

"Don't seem to want to talk much," Gabriel noted.

Hewson lay still, eyes fixed on the ceiling.

"This place won't grow on you," the lieutenant said, "so there's no worry of that."

"A small favor," Hewson said.

"Got to take 'em where you can get them," Allan said. "You play music? Me, too."

"What instrument?"

"Trumpet."

"You play, Gabe?"

"No, nothing. Well, I kind of fiddle around with my navel," he joked. "But I *am* a good listener."

"I know what you guys are trying to do," Hewson said, "and I appreciate it. But I want to be left alone, please."

***

Hewson was sitting on the back porch of his parent's place in the suburbs of Washington, D.C. It was a humid day, the air heavy and sticky. Some neighbors were playing rock music just a little too loud, and, even though they sounded like they were enjoying it, they didn't do the songs any favor by singing along.

He walked over to the glass sliding doors that led into the house. Locked. He tried knocking on the door, but when his hand hit the glass there was no sound. He grabbed the handle and pulled hard, trying to rattle the door. Again, no luck. The door didn't even jiggle.

Pressing his face against the window, he saw two figures in full dress uniform, standing behind the couch with their backs to him, at parade rest, hands behind their backs and legs slightly apart. He tried banging again. No sound. The phone rang and he saw his mother get up and take a few reluctant steps to reach for it. His father stood, face ashen and somber, at the sound of the phone. Hewson again grabbed the handle of the sliding glass doors and this time it slid open, still without sound. No one noticed him enter the room.

"Yes, this is Katherine Hewson," he heard his mother say.

"Oh." And she started to cry. "That is so wonderful," she said weakly through her tears. "Thank you so much." She hung up, holding onto the phone "James is awake and cranky." She laughed and cried. His father held her close, putting his chin on her shoulder. The two other figures turned.

"Thank you for staying with us," his father said. "Our boy is awake."

Hewson looked at the two figures: McCafferty and Craft. They nodded to his parents, glanced at him, giving the thumbs up, turned and vanished out the front door.

Hewson opened his eyes; it was dark in the ward.

"James," Gabriel said in the darkness. "McCafferty and Craft never left your side."

FIFTEEN

Lance Kirkland arrived at the air base in Germany early in the morning; it was gray and overcast with a damp chill to the air. He picked up his bags and walked off the plane.

"Chaplain Kirkland?" A young soldier greeted him at the bottom of the stairs.

"Yes," Lance returned the salute.

"I'm here to take you to the hospital."

"Lead the way," Kirkland said.

They walked across the airfield through the airport, out the front door and into a green Army sedan. Lance sat in the front on the passenger's side.

"It's not far, chaplain," the soldier explained. "What's life like back in the world?" He smiled. "You know, back in the States?"

"I can't tell you about forty nine of them, but Arizona is pretty much the same: hot and dry."

It took only a couple of minutes for them to reach the front of a long, four-story building. Lance got out, took his bags, and went in. At the reception desk, he asked for Nurse Nancy Savard.

"Chaplain," a sergeant said quietly, "we don't have a *Nurse* Savard."

Lance thought for a moment. "Well, she is also a psychiatrist."

The sergeant looked at the computer screen again.

"Yes, Dr. Nancy Savard," he said. "I'll call."

Lance stood to the side and waited.

"There is no answer, chaplain."

"I can probably find my way."

"No, sir, we will get someone to escort you," he said.

Lance realized this was polite security. "That will be fine," he answered.

Moments later, a woman corporal stood before him. "I'm heading over that way, Chaplain," she said. "Would you follow me?"

He followed the silent officer—who, he noted, was also armed—into the shadowy gray corridor that led to Nancy's office.

"Dark," he observed.

"This section is not used much," she said. "The corridors are kept dark to conserve energy."

"Even at night?"

She pointed to the small, plastic shields that were positioned near the floor and spaced a few feet apart. "Those come on at night," she said. "This is Dr. Savard's office; it appears she is not in."

"I can wait here," he told her.

The soldier smiled thinly and turned to retrace her steps.

Lance felt a slight chill in the air but enjoyed it, considering the heat he had just left in Arizona. The sound of opening doors came from a different end of the corridor; he heard footsteps and saw a female figure turn a corner and start walking toward him. She was almost on top of him before he was sure it was Nancy.

"Lance?" she said.

"Hi, Nancy."

"You … what … okay, I'm surprised."

"Me, too," he said.

She opened the door to her office and they both stepped in.

"Big office … and flowers?"

"This section isn't used much. I had my choice of offices on this floor. I like the space and, of course, the room was designed for flowers."

"Impressive."

"Okay, what's up?" She sat on the couch, away from the flowers.

Lance settled on the chair next to the couch and shared that the commander of the air base in Arizona witnessed an interaction between dead Roy Johnson and his wife, explaining in detail, and also telling her what he'd heard about Joe Williams.

Nancy listened intently, then said, "What does the commander want you to do here?"

"He never defined it. I guess he just wants me to see what's going on."

"I could have given you all the information you needed by phone."

"I realize that. Remember, you did call me," he said.

"Yes, and aside from my questions, I'm glad you're here."

"Well, I'm not sure what good I'll do. But I would like to tag along and sit in on your interviews for a few days."

"Why don't you come with me to the ward right now?"

"What ward?"

"The ward in which some of the men who are reporting these experiences are healing."

On the way, she gave Lance a quick briefing on the different enlisted men and officers and their injuries. When they walked into the ward, the men were sitting around Hewson's bed. Gabriel spotted Nancy and smiled.

"What is this, a union meeting?" Nancy joked.

"Local 911, Military Juvenile Minds Chapter," Gabriel said.

"We are adamant in our juvenile tendencies," Dan Stiles said, falling into the spirit of the exchange.

"This is Lance Kirkland," Nancy said, smiling.

"Chaplain?" Allan said, "Where are you from?"

"Arizona," Kirkland responded, "though I like the weather here better this time of year."

"Dan and I are colleagues," Nancy told the group. "We've worked together before."

"I bet," Gabriel added. "Can you give any details?"

"You boys need to grow up," she admonished.

"Not as long as we have this union," the lieutenant quipped.

"I called Dan a few days ago, and shared what some of you have related to me. He's interested."

The chaplain told them what had happened in the hangar, and that the base commander was interested and had asked him to investigate further.

"You seem to be open with all this, Chaplain, or are you not telling us everything?" the lieutenant said.

"I'm not sure what else there is to tell. If this is a collection of ghost stories, it's the most unusual we've heard."

"Who does the base commander report to?" the lieutenant wanted to know.

"Someone in the Pentagon, I suppose. Are you thinking this is coming from someone higher up?"

"Why would a base commander be interested in, as you say, ghost stories, let alone have enough pull to send you half way around the world to check it out for him?"

"Well, James," Nancy interrupted, "you settling in?"

Hewson gave a slight smile and nodded briefly.

"We were just talking about the two soldiers standing by his bed every night," Gabriel said.

The lieutenant cleared his throat. "I don't care," Gabriel told him. "I've got no secrets."

"Soldiers?" Kirkland asked.

"Chaplain, every night there are soldiers in the room with us. Craft and McCafferty stand by Hewson's bed while he's sleeping."

"How do you know who they are?"

"They gave me descriptions," Hewson told him. "I recognize them by those descriptions."

"Have you seen them?"

"No, sir, but I have seen Johnson and Williams standing by Gabe's bed," Hewson answered.

"Johnson? The man I saw in Arizona?"

"Yes," Gabriel said.

"Do they say anything?"

"Nope, just stay by us, like they're on duty, standing watch," Allan said. "The only time they're not here is when someone leaves the ward."

"When they go home?"

"Or die," Allan said quietly.

"Would you mind if I spent some time in the ward over the next few nights?"

"I'm not sure, Chaplain. You got a union card?" Gabriel asked.

SIXTEEN

Marsharaf lay in the sand on his stomach, watching a long line of tanks pass. He counted seventeen, all traveling in the same direction, spread out across the open terrain. He had to choose which to attack in order to do the most damage. These tanks were not to gain easy access to the next town.

Mugabe was next to him, holding two canvas bags containing enough explosives to blow up one of the tanks and hopefully send small bits of shredded metal into the other surrounding tanks. With a little luck, they could disable four or five of the vehicles.

Marsharaf tapped Mugabe on the shoulder as the line of tanks rumbled past them. He pointed to the second closest they started to run. Mugabe was the first to reach their goal, tossing one of the explosive bags back to Marsharaf. They placed the explosives underneath the moving tanks and then began to run back.

Bullets started hitting all around them, some close enough to sting their feet. Marsharaf grabbed his left arm and chest at the same time Mugabe dropped face first into the dirt, not moving. More shots, then the explosion.

***

Mugabe did not recognize his surroundings. The brightly painted structures had more colors than he had ever seen. He walked along a hard, dark surfaced road, passing house after house and feeling strangely out of place, his worn shoes not making a sound.

He crossed the street at the corner toward a long, one-story brick building that had many gray metal lined windows. Brightly dressed children played in a fenced in field at the far end. This was not his country; no children there had clothes like this. He walked up to the fence, unnoticed by the children or the two women with them.

A man in dress uniform stood at the far end of the small field observing the children at play. When Mugabe looked closely, he noticed the man was not watching the children but was looking at the women. A ball rolled over to them and the petite, brown haired young woman picked it up. While throwing it back, she noticed the man in uniform. A look of surprise flooded her face and she ran to the soldier, throwing her arms around his shoulders and burying her face in his chest. She pulled back, tears flowing, to study the man. Again, she pulled him to her, laying her head against him and wiping her eyes.

Mugabe wiped a tear from his cheek.

The sound of a vehicle came from behind him. He turned to see a green car, from which two soldiers emerged. Mugabe thought to hide, fearful that they were coming for him, but quickly realized they were going into the building. He followed.

A woman standing behind a counter in the office was the first to notice the two soldiers. Then the others became still, apprehension visible in their expressions.

The woman behind the counter greeted the soldiers and nodded, then walked over and knocked on a door in the back of the room.

An older man stepped out, his face reflecting worry and shock as the woman pointed to the soldiers while saying something. He raised his arm, indicating for the two soldiers to come into his office. They spoke for a moment and the man told the woman something. Mugabe heard a name: Michael Straus. The woman's face lost all color. She nodded, put her head down and departed, grabbing tissues to wipe her tears as she left. Several other women in the office, realizing what was occurring, put their faces in their hands, struggling with their emotions.

Soon, the woman Mugabe had noticed with the soldier outside entered the office. She was trying to tell everyone she was okay. She nodded a lot and held their hands as if consoling them. The man opened the door and waved for the woman; Mugabe followed her. She greeted the two officers, smiling and shaking her head. She was pointing to a wall at the far end of the room, but indicating something outside the wall.

One of the officers opened an envelope and handed her some metal tags, a small crucifix, and a picture. Her eyes opened wide in recognition and she started crying, still shaking her head, as one of the soldiers put his arm around her in an attempt to calm her and get her to sit. She straightened and pushed him away, throwing the tags at the other officer before running out of the room.

Mugabe followed her as she ran down a long hallway, pushing her way through two gray doors and out onto the field. The children in the yard stopped their games to watch her run, knowing without knowing how that something terrible had happened.

She stopped, falling to her knees at the place where the soldier had embraced her, her face twisted in pain. She turned from left to right, putting her hand up to her head, crying his name, Michael, over and over. The man and the two women came up to her. Again, she pushed them away, shaking her head against their attempts to calm her. She collapsed on the ground in a fetal position, still shaking her head in denial.

***

Private Michael Straus stopped his tank at the sound of the gunfire. He turned to see two men run across the field behind him and then fall face first in the sand.

It was very hot, heat shimmering off the cement, as Straus walked alone along a row of brown, dusty buildings. Picking one at random, he entered, passed through, and exited in the rear, where he found an old man sitting on a splintered wooden crate in the shade of the building, his face dusty with gray stubble. A white hat with a dark sweat ring sat low over his eyes. He sipped occasionally from the canvas sack that lay near his feet. A sandy dust cloud, lifted from the ground by a passing car, slowly moved toward him.

Straus studied the old man for a long moment before crossing to stand in the shade next to him.

Across the street and just down the road, a dark-skinned young man walked hurriedly in their direction. The old man squinted, trying to see the approaching visitor, then shifted awkwardly on the crate and then struggled to his feet. He smiled widely as tears ran down his face, leaving tracks in the dust that had settled there. He waved enthusiastically to the young man, encouraging him to quicken his pace. The two embraced and the young man stepped back, keeping his hands on the old man's shoulders.

Straus saw another dust cloud: an Army vehicle, kicking up more dust and sand as it went past, causing the old man to gesture angrily. But the young man's face remained peaceful even when looking at the vehicle. A knock came at the door and the old man complained while walking into the house to answer it. While he was gone, Straus met the young man's eyes. The peace he felt was profound.

Angry words from inside distracted him and he turned to watch the old man lead two enemy officers through the house. Ducking to avoid being seen, Straus watched as the officers came through the back door, seeing no one. They looked at the old man, who had followed them through the door and was looking, obviously perplexed, around the empty space.

SEVENTEEN

Kirkland went to Nancy's office after finding a small room in the hospital in which to leave his belongings.

"Working late?" he asked her, looking at the clock that read just after eight.

"Thought I'd hang around to see what you're going to do," she said.

"So, you are going to watch me watch?"

"Just like old times," she said.

"What do you think these men are experiencing?"

"Officially? It's trauma stress; fairly common."

"Unofficially?"

"Things are changing, Lance. There are many, many indications telling us to stop and move in other directions."

"These ghost stories are telling us we have to change," he said, barely able to hide his irritation. "What time is lights out?"

"2200."

"I'm hungry. Where can I get something to eat?"

She led him down a level to a small cafeteria. "Probably not much more here than a cheese sandwich at this time of day," she informed him.

"I don't care."

Lance picked out a small salad and some chicken pieces and carried his scant meal to a table in a dimly lit corner.

"It's more than ghosts telling us to change," Nancy stated. "People are feeling it; it's everywhere."

"Come on, Nancy," he said. "These are wartime stories we've heard before—Bosnia, Desert Storm, Vietnam."

"Yes, Vietnam. What about the reports of the KIA in the peace demonstrations, showing up on the floor of political conventions? People got spooked."

"Right, spooked by spooks. Nothing was ever documented."

"Nothing that we can get our hands on," she parried. "The same old thing: 'How do we document a spook?'"

"Look, I'm here to get information for a commander. I was not told what to look for, so it's a fact finding trip. But I can tell you I am not going back with some anti-war ghost stories."

"Because you believe war is necessary."

"Because I believe in good and evil and evil has to be fought."

"So you can kill the devil with a bullet? The people we're fighting, believe we're the evil ones, remember? We've invaded and are destroying their country."

"They are wrong."

"We are all wrong," she said.

"Isn't this where we always leave off?" Lance asked, referring to earlier, unresolved debates.

"Yes, Lance. Nothing has changed. We're still fighting."

"There are still bad guys."

"And we're counted among them," she said quickly.

He held up his hand. "Okay, okay. I need us to be open with each other, so let's drop the subject. We need communications, not trenches."

"And why won't that work on an international level?"

He shrugged, not having an answer.

They walked in silence through the corridor to the quiet, darkened ward where they seated themselves at a desk that had three chairs. Lance sat in one and Nancy chose another two seats away.

"Demilitarization zone?" he asked, pointing to the chair between them.

She didn't look at him. "Just what I thought," he said under his breath.

Nancy put her finger to her lips then pointed to the other end of the ward. A flash of light reflecting off something metallic shined across the room, falling on Lance's face. Two soldiers in full dress uniform were standing facing each other next to one of the beds, their faces expressionless.

"Whose bed is that?" Lance reached across and touched Nancy on the sleeve.

"Gabriel Gordon's."

Nancy tried to stop him as he walked toward the bed at the end other of the ward. When he got within a few feet of the bed, one of the soldiers came to attention, turned, took a step forward, and faced the chaplain. Kirkland slowed as he recognized the soldier as the same he'd seen in the hangar in Arizona. As he stepped cautiously toward the bed, the other soldier came to attention, turned, took one step forward and also faced the chaplain.

Lance watched both soldiers watch him.

After a long moment, one solder turned and went back to his position by the bed. The other soldier did the same thing.

Nancy stood at the foot, with soldiers on either side. Another flash. They turned to see two different soldiers standing next to another bed.

"Whose bed is that?"

"Hewson's."

They approached Hewson's bed and the same events reoccurred: the soldiers acknowledging their presence, and then. The same routine recurred beside the beds of Allan, Jeff, and Dan.

Nancy touched the chaplain on the arm and nodded toward the chairs at the front of the ward. They watched for hours. The soldiers never moved.

Just after midnight, a nurse entered the ward. Nancy met her and gave instructions that she proceed with her rounds. With them watching, the nurse went to each bed, checking the patients. As she approached, the soldiers moved to the head of the bed, as if trying to stay out of her way.

Nancy and Lance followed the nurse out of the ward after she finished her rounds.

"Nurse," Lance called to her, "did you see those soldiers?"

"Yes," she said. "They are here every night."

"Do you report it?"

"To whom?" the nurse questioned. "This isn't unusual. It happens a lot."

"What happens a lot?"

"Guards at the bed of wounded soldiers," she said.

"It happens in the other wards?"

"Yes. My mother and grandmother were military nurses and they often talked of similar experiences."

"But," Nancy started, "I thought—"

"They told me they saw it occasionally," the nurse continued, "but not as much as I see it."

"And you still don't report it?" Nancy repeated the question.

"To whom? No one wants to know," the nurse said over her shoulder as she walked away.

"I'm going to check the other wards," Nancy said.

Each ward they walked into had two soldiers by every bed, all in dress uniform. At every bed they were met by both soldiers, acknowledged—or recognized—and then the soldiers would return to their posts.

In the last ward they entered, there was not an empty bed. The room seemed overflowing with soldiers in dress uniforms. At the front of the ward, just after they came in, Lance and Nancy were met by an officer who the insignia of general on his shoulders. Walking directly up to them so forcefully that they both took a step back, he stared at them intently before returning to his original position.

This ward was actually overcrowded with men who really did not have a severe physical injury but, rather, suffered from stress-related concerns. The ward was so crowded with beds that there was hardly enough room to walk between them. As Nancy and Lance passed through, they were met over and over again by soldiers walking smartly up to them. They stopped each time a soldier approached and did not move until the soldier went back to his position.

They finished with the last ward by three am. then went back to their starting place in the ward where Gabriel and the others were. The soldiers were in the same positions at the foot of each bed.

Just before six a.m., when the activity in the corridors picked up with the change in shifts and morning meals being delivered, an orderly entered the ward, nodded to Nancy and Lance, and looked down the row of beds. The soldiers looked at him and were gone.

Lance and Nancy caught up with the orderly in the corridor.

"Sirs?" he responded.

"What did you see in that ward?" Nancy asked.

"The same thing I see very morning, ma'am," he said. "Two soldiers by each of the beds. I wait for them to recognize me and then I deliver the breakfast."

"How long has this been going on?" Lance asked.

"Long before I got here, from what I understand."

"Do you report it?" Nancy asked.

"Report what?" His attitude was one of mild irritation. "That soldiers are looking out for soldiers? Don't you think somebody should?"

Nancy and Lance walked quietly back to her office.

"What does this all mean?" Lance asked "Is it just ghosts that don't realize they're gone?"

"I bet you each of those 'ghosts' have the same story to tell. They were killed in action, went back to ease their loved ones' grief, and are still carrying out their duty."

"Their duty?"

"I believe, in combat, a soldier learns a new thing about loyalty and patriotism, and that is to protect their brothers, their comrades. And this is what they're doing."

"That is a wild theory, Nancy," Lance scoffed. "What we have here is a ghost story, a haunting. How many men have died in this ward?"

"That first solder by Gabriel Gordon's bed, did you recognize him?"

"Yes, it looked like the soldier I saw in Arizona."

EIGHTEEN

Mid-morning at the White House, the president was in the Oval Office when one of his aides came in from a briefing.

"What is this?" the President asked.

"It is the casualty report from the war," the aide responded.

"I am very aware of that. What is this addendum?" The aide looked uncomfortable at the President's question. "Well?" the President repeated.

"That section is a report on Post Action Civilian Contact, PACC."

"PACC? What is post-action civilian contact?" The President was getting annoyed.

"We are receiving increasing reports about KIAs contacting their loved ones," the aide explained.

"Ghost stories are being reported to the president?" the president asked, almost shouting. "I'm wasting my time on ghost stories?" The aide was silent but his eyes narrowed at the president's response. "Well?"

"Sir, these are not isolated occurrences; we're getting these reports daily."

"Don't these things happen in every war?" the president asked, paging through the report.

"Not at this rate, sir. We've kept records as far back as the Civil War but nothing—no other war—has had this many. The percentages are much higher than any previous war."

"And?"

"Nothing, sir."

NINETEEN

"How did you get my name?" Jane Craft spoke, irritated, into the phone.

"I received a letter from a soldier my husband served with," Cindy Johnson told her.

"Who?"

"Gabriel Gordon."

"And how would he know me?" Jane snapped.

"James Hewson is a patient in the ward in Germany. Both he and Gabriel are in the same ward, healing from war wounds."

"I'm sorry, but I still don't get the connection," Jane stated.

"Mrs. Craft," Cindy spoke very softly, "James relayed a story about a bus ride in the mountains and then a walk up a hill to a small white house with blue trim." She paused, hearing the sudden intake of breath.

"Go ahead," Jane recovered enough to respond.

"He said that you got off the bus, refusing to look at a soldier standing at the stop. And then the soldier and Hewson followed you up the hill to that small house."

"I did not see anybody but Clifford," Jane whispered into the phone.

"I don't know how he knows, Mrs. Craft, but that's not the only thing."

"I am still not following what you are trying to tell me," Jane stated after Cindy recounted several stories.

"There's something here. Yes, these men may just be trying to comfort us before we get the news, but ..."

"But?"

"But I think there could be more," Cindy finished.

"Why?"

Cindy told her about the soldiers standing next to the beds in the ward all night long and how they only left when their charge left—or died.

"I want to do some research on these types of occurrences, looking at other wars, and I'd like your permission to use your experience."

"These things have happened in previous wars?"

"Apparently so."

"Can't you just leave it alone?" Jane asked. "This could bring up so many painful memories for so many grieving people and those who have come yet to terms with their loss."

Jane looked out the window of her home across the road to the lake. There were two men walking up the road.

"Mrs. Craft?" Cindy asked.

Jane couldn't make out who they were, but continued to watch them. As they got closer, she could tell they were in uniform.

"Mrs. Craft, are you still there?" Cindy asked.

Jane breathed deeply as she watched the two soldiers march up the road. She gasped as she recognized one.

"Mrs. Craft? Mrs. Craft, is everything all right?"

Jane didn't recognize the second soldier walking at the same pace, but there was no mistaking Clifford. They turned into her driveway and walked toward the house, stopping at the bottom of the steps.

"I'm here, Mrs. Johnson." Jane spoke through her sobs. "Clifford and another soldier are standing right outside my front door."

"Roy's been coming to our home every morning since I saw him in the hangar," Cindy her. "I still think they're trying to tell us something."

"Mrs. Johnson, you may use my experiences in your research and please let me know if there's anything else I can do to help."

"Thank you. For now, can you describe what this other soldier looks like?"

From the description of the second soldier, Cindy guessed he could be Steve McCafferty, the pilot of the helicopter.

"I'll write back to Gabriel Gordon to see if he can confirm that's who it is," Cindy said. They exchanged further condolences and ended the conversation.

Jane stayed at the window, looking at her son. The second soldier turned to walk back down the driveway while Cliff remained. She waved to him; he took off his hat, nodded, and then turned, following the other soldier down the driveway and down the road.

TWENTY

Ever since Steve had shown up, John McCafferty had not slept well; the news of Steve being killed just didn't fit with what he'd seen. Steve had been here; he was sure of it. The Army had to have it wrong.

Now this letter had arrived with James Hewson's signature at the bottom; he and Steve had served together on that helicopter. How had Hewson known the details of what he'd experience just before the Department of Defense came with that crazy news?

This Hewson was writing from a hospital ward in Germany, recovering from the same event that took Steve. How could anyone in Germany know what happened here, especially someone confined to a medical ward?

He picked up the letter and read it again, thinking maybe he should contact Jane Craft, the mother of the other boy who was killed with Steve. But he wasn't sure what that would accomplish, either.

He put the letter down as the mail delivery truck pulled up to his mailbox, then went to retrieve the day's mail, which was mostly junk—flyers and notices of some carnival in town—along with the electric bill. He walked back to his porch and dropped the stack on the table next to Hewson's letter. A small, letter fell out to the side. *It must have been tucked away in one of the flyers,* John thought. The return address was from someone named Cindy Johnson. The only Johnsons he knew lived in the next county over and, as far as he could remember, none of them were named Cindy.

Cindy Johnson introduced herself as the wife of a soldier killed in battle, apologizing for writing, and sincerely expressing any regret or hurt the subject matter of the letter may cause. She explained the experience she had with her husband coming to her just moments before she got the news from the Department of Defense that Roy, her husband, had been killed in action. She also explained that Roy's parents experienced something similar before her call to them. The rest of the letter went into a bit of detail about another soldier killed in action named Joe Williams and his visit to his brother's tavern in Seattle. Then she mentioned Sergeant Gabriel Gordon and James Hewson. *The same Hewson?*

Sergeant Gordon, who was in the same hospital ward as Hewson, had contacted her with what he knew about Johnson and Williams and that Hewson had similar experience with Steve McCafferty and Clifford Craft.

John compared the names with the letter from Hewson. Clifford Craft died with Steve.

Cindy Johnson closed by asking if there was some way she could speak to him by phone.

John grumbled after reading the last paragraph. "I don't want to talk to no one about any ghost stories." He dropped the letter on the stack of mail, took his glasses off and rubbed his eyes. When he took his hands away, he could see the blurry image of someone standing in the dirt driveway next to his old pickup. He stood up, slowly putting his glasses on. It was Steve, dressed as he'd been the last time he'd come. John moved slowly to the edge of the porch, looking at his grandson. At the end of the driveway on the road was another soldier standing watching them.

Steve took of his hat and stared at his grandfather, who said nothing. Then Steve nodded, turned, and walked to the end of the driveway, and the two soldiers walked together in step down the dirt road.

John started down the steps as he saw Steve turn and walk away. He tried hard to catch up with him but, no matter how fast he tried to walk, he could not reach him. When he got to the road, they were already a good way in the distance. As quickly as he could, he got to his pickup, started it, and drove down the road. He couldn't find them. He caught up with the mail truck and flagged it to slow down.

"Afternoon, John," the driver said.

"Merle," John asked, "have you seen anyone walking this road today?"

"Nope, too hot for me to be driving, let alone walking. You looking for someone?"

John thought for a moment. "Well, I thought I saw someone walking, so I came out thinking they could use a ride. Thanks."

When John got back to his house, he picked up the letter. He sat at his desk, pulled out some paper, and began writing to Cindy Johnson.

TWENTY-ONE

Nancy sat in her office thinking about the events of the previous day. *What did we see? Ghosts? What was going on? How could so many people witness these soldiers and not say anything, just taking it in stride? Should we report it to someone? Who would I report what I saw last night? How would I write it up?* There had to be someone who has heard of this type of phenomenon, she reasoned, somewhere, but she didn't know where.

She got up from the desk to leave her office; the gray corridor felt chilly as she opened her office door. Walking out and toward the ward, she heard something behind her and turned to see the silhouette of someone standing on the far end of the corridor. It was too far away to make out who it was.

"Lance?" she called out. The figure did not move, so she walked toward it.

"Lance, this is not a good time to start playing jokes."

The figure turned and walked away, down the corridor and around a corner. She walked faster, trying to catch up. But whoever she'd seen had vanished. She checked some of the empty offices in the corridor but all the doors were locked.

She started back to the ward, looking over her shoulder ever few seconds.

"That was not Lance," she said out loud.

She entered the ward she wanted, the same one where she and Lance had begun and ended last night's vigil, the one with Gabriel Gordon. It was quiet; the men were in their beds either reading or writing. She walked over to Gabriel.

"Afternoon, Gabe," she said.

"Oh, hi." He turned his pad upside down.

"Letter home?" she asked. He nodded. "The chaplain and I sat in here last night while you were all sleeping," she told him.

"Oh, Nurse Nancy, how kinky!" Gabriel pulled the sheet up to his neck. Allan laughed and Nancy smiled

"We wanted to find out if we could see the soldiers by each of your beds," she said. Gabriel looked at her, his head tilted slightly and a question in his eyes. She held his eyes with hers, neither of them saying anything.

"Okay," he said, "I'll blink first. What did you see?"

"We saw what you all say you see."

She explained what they'd experienced. Allan was listening intently. The lieutenant got out of bed and tapped on Hewson's mattress, indicating they should join in the discussion.

"We're perplexed," she said.

"'Perplexed' is an interesting choice of words," Gabriel responded.

"Well, it's a good word for those of us who are seeing something we don't understand," she said.

"And you want us to explain it?" the lieutenant asked.

"I actually want to discuss it and give you all my impressions—and have you give me yours," she said, seriously.

"Okay" Allan said. "You go first."

"Suspicious?" she asked.

"Nah," Gabriel said. "You're an officer—sorry, lieutenant—and a psychiatrist. There's nothing to be suspicious of."

"Well, if I must go first," she said, "these soldiers were as real as you and I are here, right now. They were as if on watch, on duty, standing a post and being very observant. They didn't know the chaplain and me, and studied us as we walked by each of your beds. But, oddly, when the duty nurse came in on her midnight rounds, they let her by as if they knew her, seeming to move out of her way so she could do her work. Even when the morning orderly came in, there was no problem. And, at that point, the soldiers disappeared."

"Well, what do you make of it?" Hewson asked.

"Nothing but questions. Why, who, how?"

"How about duty?" Allan Proposed.

"Duty to what? If it's true what you men are telling us, these soldiers are dead. So why do they still feel a sense of duty?"

After a few seconds, Gabriel spoke, "I don't know, and I really would like to. When I've seen them at night, they never respond to me."

"The ones by your bed?"

"It seems," the lieutenant said, "we don't see the ones by our beds, just the ones by the other beds."

"You still don't see your soldiers?" All the men shook their heads.

"Just to let you know, this is not the only place it's happening. They're in other wards, too. The most crowded is the one with trauma stress patients."

"PTSS?" Gabriel asked.

"Yes. Another thing I thought was odd," she added, "is that the nurses and orderlies also see these soldiers and don't report it."

"They see them?" Allan asked

"That's what they tell me."

"Who would they report them to?" Hewson snickered, almost in a whisper.

"Right," the lieutenant spoke up. "What would they say, and who would they say it to? Did you report what you saw? Anyone reading a report like that would have the nurse or orderly sent for a psych eval."

"So what do we do?" Gabriel wanted to know.

"I really don't know, but we will keep talking about it," she said and walked away. Gabriel watched her and turned his pad back over. He was writing a letter to John McCafferty.

"I think she means well," the lieutenant said, "but whatever's going on could be quieted by whomever she reports to."

"Why would they do that?" Hewson asked.

"I dunno, maybe for the same reason that this has been going on for a long time and they just call it ghost stories."

"You get an answer from Cindy Johnson?" Allan asked Gabriel.

"Not yet. Might be too much for her at this point. I can't imagine what's going through her mind with all this."

TWENTY-TWO

Nancy walked down the darkened corridor to her office, slowing a bit when she saw a silhouette coming toward her.

"You look like you've seen a ghost," Lance Kirkland said.

"I thought it might be," she said seriously. They went into her office. "I just spoke with the men in the ward: Hewson, Gabriel, Stiles, Baker and Allan."

"About?"

"What we saw last night," she said.

"Are you crazy?" Lance stood and began pacing.

"Is this some kind of military secret? So secret that we keep it from the men who know more about it than we do?"

"What did you expect to gain from such a conversation?"

"Trust, openness—maybe a hell of a lot more than by not talking to them."

"What did you tell them?"

"Everything we did last night, including the PTSS ward."

"I don't understand your reasoning," he said.

"And I don't understand yours," Nancy almost shouted.

"What did they tell you?"

"Not much more than I already know. It was me telling them. I want to understand this."

"It could be nothing more than ghost stories," he said.

"And you want to keep secrets from ghosts?"

Lance stood up and walked over to the flowers. While he was looking down, Nancy noticed someone walking slowly, almost stiffly, in the corridor outside of her office. Almost immediately, another figure walked by in the opposite direction. Then the first one moved again, making it appear as though these two figures were walking back and forth in front of her office with no obvious purpose. She went to her office door, opened it and looked out: the corridor was empty. She walked the length of corridor without seeing anyone and returned to her office.

"What was that about?" the chaplain asked.

"Not sure." Nancy let the office door close behind her.

"You just get up and walk the corridor for exercise?"

Nancy again saw the figures moving in the corridor, walking back and forth, slowly, in front of her office. She pointed to the windows. Lance turned.

"What?"

"You don't see them?" she asked, surprised.

"See? See whom?"

"There are two men walking back and forth in front of my office," she told, pointing again to the window.

Lance walked over to the door, opened it, and walked out. Nancy could see him standing in front of the window, looking left and right. The two figures continued to walk back and forth, almost bumping into him.

"There is no one out there," he said.

"Okay."

"So, what's next?" he asked.

"At this point, I'm not sure. I would like to talk with every soldier who reports, or even whispers, anything similar."

"Why? What would that accomplish?"

"Therapy. I *am* a doctor," she answered, as she rose and walked to her office door.

"Where are you going?" Lance asked.

"PTSS ward."

"Why?"

"Why not?"

"With the stress those soldiers have experienced, how could we rely on anything they say?"

"I can talk with them anyway. You coming?"

Kirkland nodded.

She entered the crowded PTSS ward and approached the nurse sitting at the desk near the door. The nurse browsed through some folders and added pages to a clipboard; then she looked up and recognized Nancy.

"Dr. Savard?"

"Hi," Nancy responded.

"You don't usually come to this ward," the nurse stated.

Nancy looked at the nurse's badge. It read Jean Wilson. "Jean," Nancy said, "we'd like to talk with the men in here about paranormal phenomenon." She explained what was going on in the other wards and what she'd seen the night before. "How well do you know each case?"

"Well, none of them," Jean said.

"Who talks the most?"

Jean thought about Nancy's question for a moment. "Probably Fred Kidder." She pointed to a man sitting on his bed, laughing with some other men.

"How does he react to strangers?"

"They're all a bit suspicious," Jean explained, "but Fred talks the most"

Nancy and Lance approached Fred. The men around him saw them coming and, one by one, moved away, slowly, not looking back. Fred's smile vanished. He watched Nancy closely as she approached.

"Fred?"

"Nurse?"

"Nancy Savard." She put her hand out and then pointed to Kirkland. "Chaplain Lance Kirkland."

"How are you feeling?" Lance asked in greeting.

"Well, I'm not ready to be running laps but I could be worse," Fred told them.

"You have time for conversation?" she asked.

"I'd check my schedule, but I don't have one. I can probably squeeze you in."

Nancy explained the stories she'd been hearing from the men in the other wards. Then she went into the detail of what the loved ones back home had experienced and even had Lance explain the occurrence in the hangar.

"You do hear some weird stuff," Fred admitted.

"The chaplain and I were here late last night," she said. "We went to each ward that had soldiers. In each ward and by each bed that had a man in it, there were two soldiers. If we walked up to the beds, the soldiers would step up to meet us."

"In every ward?" Fred asked.

"In every bed that was occupied," Nancy said, nodding.

"Odd, isn't it?" Fred responded.

"This ward was the most crowded," she stated.

"They were in here?" Fred spoke in slightly mocking surprise.

"Are you comfortable talking about this?" Lance asked.

"I'm in bed; I'm probably more comfortable than you are, Chaplain," Fred said, quickly.

Nancy looked at Lance, then back to Fred. "We could talk someplace else," she suggested.

"My place or yours, nurse?" he joked. They all laughed. "This is fine," he said.

"Okay, so let's keep going. I'm trying to find out as much about these occurrences as I can."

"For what? What would the information be used for?" Fred asked.

Lance lowered his eyes. "Maybe for nothing. But there seems to be a lot of this going on. Have you had an experience?"

Fred was quiet as he looked around the ward, his eyes moving quickly from bed to bed. "Why me?" he finally asked. "Why are you talking to me?"

"We picked someone randomly," Lance stated.

Nancy stepped a little closer to the bed and whispered to Fred, loud enough for Lance to hear. "You've been given up as a talker, soldier," Nancy admitted in an overly serious voice "We're like water; we follow the path of least resistance."

Fred laughed. "I like you," he said. "I'll tell you what I know." He paused for a second. "I was in convoy of Humvees; one of them was carrying medical personnel and supplies. The route we were taking was supposed to be safe enough—no problems, no enemy positions. Even though it was through some hilly terrain, reconnaissance reported it was clear

"We left base and were moving for about ten minutes. I was in the third Humvee with the medical unit between us and the lead. The lead Humvee turned around a small hill, and we heard an RPG go off. An instant later we saw an explosion come from over the top of the hill. The lead Humvee took a hit and blew up.

"We drove around the medical unit and took the lead, making sure the medical unit stayed behind us. They wanted to get to the lead unit but we thought, at the time, it was unsafe." Fred started to get excited.

"Two medics popped out of that vehicle and ran up to us. Things got real crazy and the medics were ordered back. But, being medics, they're deaf; all they could think about was the lead Humvee. I jumped out and ran over to them, telling my sergeant they would need some cover.

"As soon as I got out, we started taking sniper fire and it was returned by the other men in my Humvee. The medics got pinned down in a hole on the hill halfway between us and the lead Humvee; they dug in a little deeper and crawled in. I yelled at them to stay down. One of them yelled back and pointed to a marine crawling out to the lead Humvee, still moving and still trying hard to get away from the flames." Fred's voice raised a little.

"The medic was Jenny Farmer. I knew her from high school; we came from the same hometown. I told her to stay, that I'd check the marine out. Jenny protested but stayed put." His words were coming a little quicker.

"The sniper fire had stopped, so I ran up to the marine. He was breathing and responding to my questions, but he was burned badly. His name was Paul or something. I looked at the Humvee; it was burning pretty good. There were men inside but no one was moving. It was a miracle that even one person survived that." Fred's eyes were fixed as if looking at the Humvee.

"I signaled for a medic to come up and pulled something over the marine to give him some cover. Jenny must have had wings; she was there in less than a second. She examined him and told me he was bad and needed to get out of there fast. I called back to my Humvee to dispatch a helicopter to get the marine to a hospital.

"We started taking some fire." Fred's voice was rising. "I returned fire and yelled for Jenny to take cover; she ducked but stayed with the Marine. I yelled at her again to take cover. Shots were coming in faster and harder. I screamed and shot back." Fred was talking very rapidly and loudly. Lance touched Nancy on the arm, indicating that she should stop him. Nancy brushed him off.

"I don't know if I hit anyone, but the shooting stopped. When I looked back at Jenny, she was slumped over the Marine. At first I thought was just protecting him, but she didn't answer when I hollered to her. When I looked closer, I could see blood running from her side into the debris." Fred started to cry.

"I don't remember much of what happened after that. I was told they had to pry her out my arms. She was such a beautiful girl, and what a soldier."

Lance Kirkland was wide-eyed as Fred continued, wiping away tears.

"What I remember next is standing in a park. It was beautiful day, warm with a nice soft breeze moving against the leaves in the branches overhead. I recognized this park as the one in my hometown. It was pretty much empty except for some small children playing on the swings at the far end. I walked toward them.

"Some adults were sitting on the benches near the swings, talking and keeping their eyes on the kids. I recognized one of the adults as Jenny's father. On Saturdays during high school I worked at his hardware store. He looked in my direction and I waved to him, but he never waved back. I don't think he recognized me. I was wearing combat clothes—the same I wore in that firefight—but you'd think he would have thought those clothes out of place.

"Jenny had a cute son. She always showed me his newest picture when we ran into each other at base. I recognized her boy playing on the swings. Her father looked in my direction again and I waved again, but it was like he was looking through me. I turned around and saw a small soldier in full dress uniform come from the same direction I had. As the soldier got closer, I could see it was Jenny. I was so glad to see her walking I started crying. I could still see her blood on my uniform.

"She smiled at me as she walked past but never said a word. Her father was off the bench and headed toward her. They met and embraced. I don't think I ever saw a father hold his daughter that way, like he was never going to let her go. Her little boy jumped off the swing and ran over to her. She let go of her father and ran to her son, picking him up. I could tell she was crying. Both father and son appeared to be talking to her but all she would do was nod as they spoke. They all walked over to an SUV in a nearby parking lot. The father drove. Jenny helped her son into a car seat in the back. Then she looked at me and, leaving the rear door open, got in on the passenger side.

"I stepped into the car and closed the door. We drove to her father's house and were getting out of the SUV at the same time a green car pulled in behind them. Jenny's father met the two officers as they walked halfway up the driveway. They spoke briefly. He shook his head no and smiled, inviting them over to the car. He opened the passenger side door and Jenny was gone."

Fred was crying, wiping his eyes and nose.

Nancy spoke first. "Have you had any contact with Jenny's father?" she asked.

"I've tried to write to Bill, but I don't know what to say to him." Fred pointed to a pad sitting at the foot of his bed. "I mean, how do I explain what I saw?"

"You may want to keep it simple, Fred," Lance said. "Just tell him you were with Jenny when she was hit."

Nancy smiled her approval. "The chaplain makes a wonderful point. It may bring a lot of comfort to her father to know you were there."

"Did what I just told you help?" Fred asked.

"Yes, quite a lot. It fits with everything else we've been hearing," Nancy responded.

"Everyone here—well, almost everyone—has a similar story. Some of these guys can't talk, though."

"Do you have any other feelings about this?" Lance asked.

"Other feelings?"

"Observations, explanations, gut reactions?"

"Just the obvious," Fred said, letting his tears flow freely. "Why is there war?" "Chaplain," Nancy asked, "you have an answer for that one?"

"Please, Chaplain, don't repeat the company line about democracy and protecting our freedoms. There has got to be a better way."

Lance nodded, put his left hand on Fred's shoulder and shook Fred's other hand. "Let Jenny's dad know you were there," he said softly. "It will help both of you."

They left the ward. Nancy looked at Lance and noticed him wiping away a tear.

"Good suggestion on what he should say to the father," she said.

"You pinned me down," Lance said. "How can I explain war to someone who's experienced what he's been through?"

"There is no one else who deserves an explanation more."

TWENTY-THREE

Cindy Johnson was sitting in her home office writing a letter to James Hewson, She wanted to get his written account of what he saw with Craft and McCafferty. She, of course, had a lot of information on her husband, Roy, and Joe Williams, including the families' experience and Gabriel Gordon's experiences. And, every situation, down to the minutest detail, was backed up by someone else. Her experience with Roy was validated by Gabriel Gordon, as was Dave Williams' experience with Joe. *How could all of these people not miss a detail?* Getting Hewson's account would help. The phone rang.

"Good afternoon, Mrs. Johnson. This is Commander Donner. How are you doing?" "Commander?" Cindy let her surprise show. "I guess I'm doing as well as can be expected.

"And your daughter, she's well?"

"She misses her father. We both do," she answered and became quiet. She

"Mrs. Johnson, what do you think we saw in the hangar that day?" Donner asked.

The question upset her. "Commander," she said slowly, "we have discussed this. That was my husband. Now, are you trying to say you did not see him?"

"I don't know what I saw," he responded abruptly. "There is so much emotion during such times that it could have been anything."

"You mean like an 'undigested bit of beef?'" she said sarcastically.

"I am not trying to upset you, Mrs. Johnson," Donner said, stiffly.

"Well, you're not doing a very good job. Do you think I would not recognize my own husband?"

"No, ma'am, I am sure you would recognize you own husband."

"What is it you really want?"

"The purpose of my call is to find out how you're doing. The experience in the hangar has been on mind and I really don't know what to make of it."

"Take it for what it is, Commander." Cindy let the title hang on her tongue a little too long. "There are things that the military, any military, no matter how strong it says it is, cannot explain or control. My husband was in that hangar. You saw him and your chaplain saw him."

"You don't trust the military very much, do you, Mrs. Johnson?"

"Nice try, Commander. What I don't understand is your questioning of what happened. I consider it a blessing."

"Thank you very much for you time, Mrs. Johnson. And I apologize if I upset you." Donner hung up. A young officer came in.

"Get me the Defense Department in D.C.," Donner said. The call was put through immediately and Donner picked up. "General, Mrs. Johnson believes she saw her husband in her home and the hangar." He paused. "No, sir. The man I saw in uniform and the man my chaplain saw resembled Corporal Johnson quite closely." Another pause to listen before stating, "A ghost, General. I saw a soldier in full dress uniform. He was as solid a figure as I ever seen. However, he disappeared. Just shook his head to Mrs. Johnson and was gone ... No, sir, I've not seen him again."

He listened, then said, "When I talked with Dave Williams he was also convinced his brother was in the bar just before he got word from his mother about the DOD."

The aide knocked on the commander's door and Donner signaled for him to enter.

"General, may I ask you a question?" Donner looked at his aide while talking into the phone. "Thank you, sir. The stories of Johnson and Williams, are they isolated or are there more occurrences?"

He cocked his head to the right. "Why am I asking? There seems there is a lot of interest at the higher command levels ... Thank you, General." Donner hung up and looked at his aide.

"He wouldn't answer my question."

TWENTY-FOUR

Jane Craft perched on her front steps, enjoying the sunny, warm afternoon. She smiled as she watched three squirrels scamper up tree trunks and then seemingly float from branch to branch in an endless game of tag. She rubbed her dog's neck absentmindedly.

"When was the last time I played like that?" She spoke to the dog.

"It's okay," she said. "I'm not about to go climbing trees to play with the squirrels."

The dog whimpered and looked down the road. A long ways off, she saw five men too far away to recognize.

As the men drew closer, she saw they were wearing military uniforms. She bit her lip, and the dog started wagging its tail.

"There, there," she said. "Clifford is gone. You just settle down. These men don't need you bouncing all over them, getting your hair all over their uniforms." The five men walked, in single file, past the bus stop down from her house. Jane put her eyes down, not *wanting* to recognize any of them.

"They'll just keep walking by us," she said while rubbing behind the dog's ear. "Must be some kind of training exercise or maybe punishment for carousing last night." The dog barked as, one by one, the five turned and started to walk up her driveway.

"Oh, Clifford," she sobbed. "Why do you keep coming here?" The dog ran down the steps toward the approaching soldiers, barking happily but quietly as the five walked past. The soldiers came to within a few feet of Jane and stood still, eyes straight ahead. The only one looking directly at her was Clifford.

"What do you want, son?" she cried. "Why do you keep coming here?" She recognized one of the other soldiers; he'd come with Clifford on a previous occasion. But this was the first time she'd seen the other three. She was surprised when she realized one was a woman.

The phone rang. Jane rubbed her face with both hands, stood and went into the house. Suddenly the ringing seemed urgently loud. She crossed the room, picked up the receiver and took a deep breath before putting it to her ear. She stood looking at the front window, still able to see the five soldiers in her drive way.

"Hello," she said.

"Jane, this is Cindy Johnson."

"Yes, Mrs. Johnson?"

"I need to talk with someone. Dave Williams is not answering his phone. I've been alternating calling him and you."

"Yes, Mrs. Johnson," Jane whispered, suddenly realizing that her phone had been ringing repeatedly; she'd ignored it.

"Roy is here," Cindy yelled on the verge of hysterics. "He is standing here outside my window with four other soldiers."

"My Clifford is here, Mrs. Johnson, with four other soldiers. One of the soldiers is a woman. Mrs. Johnson? Mrs. Johnson?"

Cindy finally responded. "One of the soldiers here is a woman," she said. "Jane, I've got a call coming in. Do you mind if I put you on hold? Please, don't hang up."

"I'll wait," Jane assured her. She sat down on the arm of the sofa, still able to see soldiers.

***

"Hello," Cindy said.

"Cindy?"

"Yes."

"This is Dave Williams. Were you just trying to contact me?"

"Yes, Dave, I was. Roy is here with four other soldiers. I've only seen one picture of your brother but I believe Joe is one of them," she said.

"Cindy," Dave said. "Joe is here with four soldiers and I believe Roy is one of *them*." Dave was looking outside through the window of his tavern; there were four soldiers standing next to his brother, Joe. "And, Cindy, one of the soldiers is a woman."

"There's a woman here, too. I have Jane Craft holding. She has her son, who was also KIA, standing in front of her yard with four other soldiers and one of them is a woman." She paused and said, "I'll be right back."

How could the three of us, all with loved ones killed in action, be experiencing something so similar? She reconnected with Jane. "Jane, that was Dave Williams; I still have him on hold. He told me his brother, Joe, is there with four other soldiers. One he thinks is my Roy and one of them is a woman."

"Oh, God." Jane sighed. "Sweet Jesus. What does this mean?"

"I don't know, Jane. Would you mind if I give your number to Dave?"

"Please do. I think the three of us should be able to contact each other," Jane responded.

Cindy put her back on hold while she gave Dave the number, and repeating the suggestion that the three of them need to stay in touch.

"Please give her mine," he said.

"I don't know what's going on here," Cindy said, "but I can't shake the feeling that these soldiers are trying to tell us something."

"What? Why don't they stay at rest? What do they want? What can we do for them?"

"I don't know, Dave. Hold on."

Cindy switched back over to Jane, repeating Dave's question about what they could do to help the soldiers and what they wanted.

"Could there be more?"

"More?"

"Yes, could this be happening to others who've lost someone in the war?"

Cindy didn't have the answer, just a feeling she should find out.

"Looks like they're leaving," Cindy said.

"Clifford is leaving, too," Jane announced.

"Jane, I promise to call you soon," Cindy said.

"Thank you, Mrs. Johnson."

"Please, call me Cindy," she said and switched to talk with Dave.

"He's gone," Dave said before Cindy could say anything.

"Roy is gone, too, and Jane's son, Clifford, is also gone. But she said something to me about there may be being others, more people who lost someone in the war experiencing the same thing."

"How could we find that out?"

"I don't know," she said, explaining her latest correspondence with Gabriel Gordon. "I'm going to mention this in my next letter. Maybe he can give us some more connections."

TWENTY-FIVE

For some reason the ward seemed dark even though the hallway lights were on; Gabriel was barely able to see the shadowy figures by the beds around the ward. The light near the door helped him see someone — he couldn't tell who — sitting at the nurse's desk. He pulled himself up in bed, hoping for a better view.

The woman stood up, walked to the door, opened it, looked both ways down the outside corridor, closed the door, and then walked to the center of the ward. Gabriel saw different soldiers turn to her as she walked past each occupied bed. He recognized Nancy when she walked by him. She continued down to Allan's bed. One soldier, a woman, moved from the head of the bed and Nancy stopped. After a long moment, the soldier returned to Allan's side. Nancy came back to Gabriel's bed.

"Can't sleep?"

"Some nights are better than others."

"Is that normal?"

"It is since the legs got hit."

"I can get you something for the pain," she told him.

"Nah, they don't hurt much. Just the mind is too active."

"Thinking about home?"

"Thinking about home," he agreed. "Also Johnson, Williams, their families and my family. All this stuff seems to have a connection."

"How could they be connected?"

He handed her a couple of letters. "Read these and see if you don't make a connection."

"What do they say?"

He briefly explained his correspondence with Cindy Johnson and what she had been doing back home, the contacts she had made, and also her interaction with Kirkland and Commander Donner.

"Why is she doing this?"

"You're the head doctor," Gabriel said "My first thought was that she was just trying to bring closure or healing by talking with others who are going through what she's experiencing. But she makes a convincing argument about a connection."

"What have you told her?"

"Whatever she asks. She's the last person I'd hold anything back from," Gabriel said. "I tell her what I've seen, what any of us has seen, and also tell of any soldier who would like to talk with her."

"You've given her names?"

"Yep," he said, almost defiantly. "I feel obligated to help."

"I'll bring them back," Nancy said, indicating the letters.

"Chaplain Jesus doesn't buy into these ghost stories, does he?"

"Chaplain Jesus? He's trying to stay objective."

"He's seen these soldiers?"

"Yes."

"I can tell him where he can put his objectivity."

"I'll bring these back," she repeated.

"Show them to Chaplain Jesus."

***

Her office was dimly lit by the light from her desk. "What is going on?" she whispered as she read the letters that Gabriel Gordon had handed her. "What is the connection?"

"Midnight oil?" Lance asked as he walked in.

"Just thinking," she said nonchalantly, folding the letter and notes and then putting them in the top desk drawer. "What do you think is happening?"

"Here?"

"Yes."

"I'm not sure, but I'm trying to be objective," he said.

"How can you be objective? You've seen them yourself."

"Ghost stories? There has to be a rational explanation, something more that we don't know."

"These are not ghost stories and you know it."

"Could be mass hypnosis, mass hysteria," he stated.

"So, you and Donner were hysterical in the hangar that day?"

"We were definitely not objective. We both knew the story about Roy Johnson. We were with his wife. It's easy to get caught up in that kind of thing."

"With all that you've seen and experienced, you're still looking for a 'rational' explanation, a way to just explain it all away?"

"Nancy, there is no proof that these manifestations are supernatural and not the product of mass hysteria."

"Chaplain," she said dismissively, "being objective is one thing; denying what you've seen is something else."

"I'm not denying anything."

"You're not admitting anything, either," she said, thinking for a second before continuing. "Or is that part of a cover-up?"

"A cover-up?" Lance said, angrily. "What would I be covering up? For what purpose?"

"If you *are* here to help, admit what you have seen and go from there. But if you're here to gather information to pass on to someone else higher up, then please go away and stop being an obstacle to my investigation."

"An obstacle?"

"I get the feeling that if it were up to you, you'd go back to Arizona and just put this down to too many years of watching movies and reading New Age books. Lance, I don't need you here."

"Well, I'm staying."

"Then please stay out of my way."

After he'd slammed out of the room, she pulled out the letters. *Should I have shown them to him?* Her gut feeling was to keep things away from him until it became necessary. She reread the part about the five soldiers visiting the families back home. Earlier visits were one, then two; now there were five? *Mass hysteria from people living thousands of miles apart? These visitations all happening at the same time?*

TWENTY-SIX

The President's aide knocked on the door to the Oval Office and entered as he heard the president respond.

"Sir, Commander Donner's report." The aide handed him a sealed envelope.

"Thank you," the president said. The aide left the office as the president opened the envelope.

Mr. President,

Chaplain Lance Kirkland is in Germany gathering information on the phenomenon that you have inquired about. All reports are similar: servicemen killed in action are visiting their loved ones just before DOD notification. Recently we have received information that there have been multiple simultaneous visitations.

As you may be aware, the Chaplain and I experienced a manifestation of this phenomenon. Chaplain Kirkland and Dr. Nancy Savard have also seen those KIA standing near the beds of wounded men they served with. The apparitions appear to be sentient, in that they acknowledge people who approach, if only briefly. It also seems that, whatever this is, it is happening in more than one ward.

I will report further as additional information becomes available to me.

Respectfully,
Commander John Donner

TWENTY-SEVEN

Cindy Johnson dialed John McCafferty's home phone number. She had not talked to him by phone and wanted to know if his experiences were the same as hers, Jane Craft's, and Dave Williams'. She was also hoping she could get more names of others who were experiencing these things—if there were more.

"Hello." An older man's voice answered, sounding winded.

"Mr. McCafferty?

"Yes."

"This is Cindy Johnson. We've corresponded by mail."

"Yes, Mrs. Johnson. How are you and your daughter?"

"I am well and so is Carol."

"What can I help you with?"

"I know how this question must sound and I apologize in advance for any pain it will cause you, but have you seen Steve lately?"

"Seen him?"

Cindy repeated what she wrote about the experience that she had in the hangar, then the experience she had with the five soldiers in front of her place and also told him the experiences of Jane and Dave.

"In the hangar, when your husband was being returned home," John asked. "only you saw him?"

"No. The chaplain and the base commander were there and saw him, too."

"And what were their reactions?"

"When I spoke with the commander the other day, he was still questioning what he saw. At least, that's what he told me. But I have a hunch he called to try to get more information."

"Not surprising."

"Why?"

"Seems to me it would be a huge PR problem if word got out that the war dead were visiting home."

"PR problem for a war?. What an oxymoron," Cindy said.

"For a country so dedicated to peace, we sure have had a lot of wars," he said softly. "Think what would happen if it became common knowledge that the dead were not at peace."

"Mr. McCafferty, have you seen Steve since the DOD was there to notify you?"

"Yes, I have. Steve was here with four other soldiers the same day you saw your husband with four other soldiers. And one of those soldiers who was here, and with you and the others, was a woman."

"Have you told anyone else?"

"I had a call from one of the officers who delivered the news of Steve's death."

"One of the officers from the Department of Defense?"

"Yes. Said he was just checking on me. We talked for a while. He said he had a grandfather about my age and that he would want someone to check on him if he received such bad news."

"And you told him about Steve and the four other soldiers?"

"Yes," John answered.

"How did he take it?"

"Like he didn't believe it," John told her. "He left his phone number for me in case I ever wanted to just call and talk."

"Could you give it to me?"

"Sure. But why do you need it?"

"Another possible source of information," she explained.

John put the phone down and went to get the name and number of his caller.

Odd to have a call from the DOD so long after the notification, she mused as she waited. She wasn't sure she believed the 'caring serviceman' checking up on an old man who lived alone.

John got back on the phone and gave the number.

"Thank you," she said. "You do know how to contact me, right?"

"I have your address," he answered.

Cindy gave him her phone number, repeated her address, said goodbye and hung up. The phone rang almost immediately.

"Mrs. Johnson?"

"Yes?"

"This is Lieutenant Vincent Russo. I was one of the two men who gave you the news about your husband being killed in service to our country."

Cindy was very quiet, not immediately responding. She was very suspicious; why would she be contacted by the DOD now? Two caring soldiers? Not likely.

"Mrs. Johnson?"

"I'm sorry, Lieutenant, but you're probably the last person on earth I expected to get a call from."

"I understand," he said. "It's just that I know the killed in action notification was terrible for you, and I felt very bad to have to give you the news. And your experience, just before we arrived, made it even worse. I was just wondering how you and your little girl are doing."

"We're doing okay, Lieutenant. And I do appreciate your call. But is this normal procedure?"

"Is what normal procedure?"

"A follow-up contact?"

"Sometimes, ma'am. But this is really personal. I have a wife and a daughter, and your reaction touched me. I got to thinking about how they'd handle it if someone had to notify them about me."

McCafferty had a caring soldier with a grandfather and now I get the caring husband and father.

"That is very considerate, Lieutenant."

"Just out of curiosity, have you seen your husband since that day?"

"What?"

Ah, so now we get to the purpose of this call.

"What I mean is was that the only time you saw him, just before our notification?" Russo stuttered.

Cindy hesitated, still not trusting, but then decided to give him a very brief rundown of her hangar experience, including the fact that a chaplain and commander also saw her dead husband.

"So you wanted to open the coffin for proof he was dead, confirming what we told you?"

"Yes," she said quickly. She did not feel comfortable with this phone call.

"I can understand that," he responded. "But you never opened the coffin?"

"No, Lieutenant. There was no need, especially with two Army officers witnessing what I saw." She had the feeling he already knew what she was telling him. He'd likely read the reports.

"Have you seen him any other times?"

"No," she said stiffly, hoping to give the impression that he was intruding. There was no need to tell him that Roy had, indeed, visited again.

"I think this is so interesting," Russo said. "All my life I've heard stories like this in which loved ones reached out just before they crossed over."

"I have to…" Cindy let her voice trail off, hoping he'd take the hint.

"Well, Mrs. Johnson, thank you for your time. I know the subject is painful for you. If you ever want to talk, this is where you can reach me." He gave her the number.

"Thank you, Lieutenant," she said, ending the call.

She then immediately dialed Dave Williams' number. Busy. Okay, she told herself, it's a tavern. But when Jane Craft's number was also busy, she had second thoughts.

"Maybe it's a coincidence?" she whispered doubtfully.

She decided to write a letter to Gabriel Gordon, telling him about the calls that she and John McCafferty had received. She wanted more than one person to have all the information, though she still wasn't sure why.

Her phone rang. It was Dave Williams.

"Dave," she said. "I just tried to call you a little while ago."

"I was on the phone with one of the soldiers who notified my mother of Joe's death," he said. Cindy listened carefully to how the soldier said he called out of concern.

"So he called because he had a brother who owned a business and would like someone to check up on his brother after such terrible news?" Cindy sounded suspicious. Her apprehensions were being confirmed.

"I got a similar call," she told him, "only mine was a soldier with a wife and daughter.

"Two caring soldiers?" Dave was skeptical. Cindy then told him about the call that John McCafferty from the soldier who 'had a grandfather'.

"So we have three caring soldiers," Dave said.

"It could happen," she said. "I guess."

"Yeah, but it just makes me so suspicious."

"Me, too," she admitted. "Like when I was trying to call you and got a busy signal. Then I tried to call Jane Craft and her phone was also busy. I wondered if you both were getting follow-up contacts."

"Did you ever get through to her?"

"No, you called me before I tried again. Did the soldiers leave a phone number for you to contact them?"

Dave gave her the number he'd been given.

"That's the same number I got," she told him.

"Well, Roy and Joe were in the same unit," Dave said. "Maybe that's how these assignments are handed out?"

"Let me check the number that John McCafferty gave me." She put the phone down. "It's the same number," she said, picking back up. "And Steve McCafferty was not in the same unit as Joe and Roy."

"Well, you're right, it is odd," Dave said. "But maybe that's just a general number that connects to everyone all over the country."

"Maybe," Cindy said "but I want to talk with Jane."

"Okay," Dave said. "I'll let you go. Let me know what is going on."

Cindy hung up and dialed Jane Craft's number.

"Hi, Jane," Cindy said as soon as the woman picked up the phone.

"Hi, Cindy. I just got off the phone with the nicest young man who called to see how I was doing," Jane said.

Cindy told her about the calls that she, Dave Williams, and John McCafferty had received.

"Did he give you any contact information?" Cindy asked. Jane gave her the number.

"That's the number we all got," Cindy said.

"Is something wrong, Cindy?" Jane asked.

"Four 'caring' soldiers, all with identical family situations as each of us, making follow-up calls, all at about the same time? And all calling people who had experienced something unusual? I'm not sure what the Army wants with this information, though. People seeing ghosts isn't new, but it also doesn't strike me as something the Army'd be interested in."

They chatted for a few more minutes before ending the call.

Cindy went to finish writing her letter to Gabriel.

She brought him up to date, and then ended with a question, asking if he knew who the woman soldier was. "How would he know that?" she said out loud, as she stuffed the letter into the envelope.

TWENTY-EIGHT

Gabriel Gordon sat on his bed, barely comfortable with his heavily bandaged legs dangling over the edge and the latest letter from Cindy Johnson in his hand. He was looking out the window.

"What's up?" Hewson asked, standing at the foot of Gordon's bed.

"Not much. Just thinking."

"You get another letter?"

Gabriel nodded. "The woman likes to write."

"I don't know if she's just doing this as part of her healing, or if she's actually onto something," Gordon said, still looking out the window. He handed Hewson the letter. "Seems like she's staying in contact with some other folk who are also experiencing seeing their loved ones, and now they're seeing groups of soldiers."

Hewson read the letter. "She says there's a woman soldier."

"I know," Gabriel responded.

"What others?"

"The two guys killed when I was hit were Johnson and Williams. Cindy Johnson has been in contact with the family of the two guys that died when you were hurt, Craft and McCafferty, and now there's a fifth soldier, a woman." Gordon looked over at Allan, who was in his bed, sleeping.

"What are you getting at?" Hewson asked.

"There's a connection and it seems to be with this ward."

"Well, what about Stiles and Baker? If the connection is with this ward, wouldn't Stiles be involved?"

"Good question." Gordon was thinking.

"So what do we do?"

Gordon explained that he'd given his other letters to Nancy, but had not heard back from her about them. "I'm not sure I should give her this one," he said.

"Why not?"

"Reread the last part." Gordon told him. "She received a follow-up call from one of the guys who gave her the KIA news."

"Seems they all got a follow-up call," Hewson remarked. "So what? The soldiers who have to give the bad news to loved ones can't be unaffected by it. They have feelings, too. And I'm sure there's always the thought that it could have been their loved ones getting the news."

"You don't think it's a coincidence that all of the follow-up calls were from someone who had the exact same family conditions and that the calls were made all about the same time?"

"So you think it's unusual to have a wife and a daughter, a brother, a mother, a grandfather? A coincidence? Seems normal enough to me," Hewson said. "And why not trust Nancy with this information?"

"I'm not sure," Gordon said. "She's been questioning everyone here and now the government's questioning the families; just seems to be a lot of interest."

"Looks like you have a decision to make, Sergeant," Hewson said as he looked over his shoulder. "Here comes Nurse Nancy and Chaplain Jesus now."

Gabriel folded the letter and slipped it under his pillow. Nancy was looking in his direction. Had she seen it? She stopped by Stiles' bed and talked with the lieutenant for a while. The conversation seemed pleasant, with Stiles nodding quite often. What did seem odd to Gabriel was that the chaplain took a seat at the desk by the door of the ward and stayed there.

"Hmm," Hewson noted, "Jesus and the nurse seem not to be playing well together today."

The conversation between Nancy and Stiles was lasting a long time. Whatever they were talking about seemed to be making the lieutenant happy. The more he nodded, the more he smiled.

"What's going on?" Allan whispered.

"We've got company," Gabriel told him. "Seems Nancy needs to talk with the lieutenant about something. They've been jawing for a few minutes now."

"You hear more from Kidder?" Hewson asked Allan.

"Not since the other day."

Hewson walked to Allan's bed and turned his back to the rest of the ward. He did not want his voice to carry. Allan leaned closer as Hewson shared the new information Gabriel had received.

Nancy put her hand out to Stiles and the lieutenant grabbed it, shaking it enthusiastically. She walked to the end of the ward, with Gabriel, James and Allan watching every step. Kirkland caught up with her just before she reached Gordon's bed.

"How are you men doing today?" she asked. Kirkland stood just close enough to hear.

"Fine, Nurse Nancy," all three of them chimed together, sounding more like school kids than soldiers. She laughed. Stiles popped up from his bed, laughing, too. The only one who didn't laugh was Kirkland, who forced a smile to his lips.

"So, what's this union meeting about?" she asked.

"Oh, the usual," Hewson said. "Wages, benefits, and ghosts." He looked at Kirkland when he said the word 'ghosts.'

"Ghosts are a union concern?" Kirkland tried to joke.

"Everything is around contract time," Hewson told him with mock solemnity.

Nancy looked at Gabriel while Hewson and Kirkland bantered. She glanced down at the pillow and Gabriel knew she'd seen him hide the letter. He tried not to act suspicious.

"Any new ghosts to report?" she asked.

"No, just the normal ones—matured and ready to retire," Gordon answered.

"How are the legs doing?" Nancy asked as she moved closer to the bed. Kirkland watched her closely.

"Talking about meetings," Gabriel said, trying to keep the conversation under some control, "was that a management meeting between you and the lieutenant?"

"Oh, I'm sure he'll let you guys know." Nancy was checking his legs.

"I can do that now," Stiles called out. "Being shipped back to the States for more treatment and then discharged!"

"Cool." Hewson clapped and whistled. "When do *we* all go back?"

"You're going to be here a while, I'm afraid. The lieutenant has specific treatment that needs to be handled back in the States."

"So it'll just be us?" Allan said.

"Yeah, you guys are special," Kirkland said jokingly. Gabriel did not take what Kirkland said as a joke. Instead, he felt the chaplain's remark had more than a little truth to it.

"Probably have to change the dressing on the left leg, Sergeant. I'll do that in a few minutes." Nancy looked at him and then at the pillow. She turned to Hewson. "I need to check your bandages, too, before I leave." She walked around to Allan's bed.

"My bandages were changed this morning," he said.

"Yes, they look fresh. How are you feeling?" she asked.

Allan responded that he was feeling better every day and feeling constant improvement, though he seemed to be sleeping more.

"You didn't sleep well when you first got here. Sleep whenever you can."

Hewson moved back to his bed. Nancy followed and started to check his bandages. She placed her hand on his shoulder and made a tapping motion and then left.

"Ah, going stateside, Lieutenant," Gabriel called out.

"Yep."

"When?"

"Seems like it could be today. She was going to check and get back to me."

"Wow, that is fast. Won't give you much time to pack," Allan joked.

"Been here four months, Allan. All I need is what's on my back." Stiles smiled and laid back.

Gabriel Gordon leaned toward Allan's bed. "Can you give me a description of Jenny," Gabriel asked in a whisper.

Allan described her as best he could, reminding Gabriel that all he had was what he'd seen in his dreams—what she looked like when she went back to see her father and son before the DOD notification. "You may want to check with Kidder. He really knew her," Allan added.

"The full dress description is probably best because all the soldiers are showing up that way. If it is really Jenny with them, this is the way she is appearing," Gabriel said, tucking Allan's written description with the letter he received from Cindy Johnson.

"You gonna send that back to the States?" Allan asked.

Gabriel handed him the latest letter from Cindy. "Go ahead, read it," Gordon said. "I'm not sure what's going on. Maybe nothing. But there seems to be quite a lot of interest in these 'ghost' stories."

Allan read the letter and then quickly handed it back. "I've never heard of a follow-up call from the DOD," he said.

"Me neither."

"And all four of these families get a follow-up call at nearly the same time? What are the odds?"

"If it's not standard procedure, very small," Gabriel said as Fred Kidder walked into the ward.

"Who let you out?" Allan called to him.

"Well, it's not who you know," Kidder responded, making a sexual gesture. "How are all you guys?"

"Good," Hewson responded. "The lieutenant is getting an all-expenses paid trip to the States."

"No kidding," Fred exclaimed, standing at the foot of the lieutenant's bed.

"That's what the nurse said. I might be out of here today."

"Must feel real good to be heading back home," Fred said, walking to the back of the ward. He stopped between Gabriel's and Allan's beds. "How are you guys?"

"Feeling better every day," Allan told him.

"I'm okay" Gabriel said.

"I just got a letter from Bill, Jenny's dad," Fred told them as he sat at the end of Allan's bed. "He says they're doing all right adjusting to Jenny being gone."

"That's good," Gabriel said.

Hewson was making his way slowly to the back of the ward.

"Yeah," Fred continued, "must be tough to lose a child."

"But?" Hewson said as he leaned against Gabriel's bed.

"What?" Fred asked.

"Sorry," Hewson said, embarrassed. "I just got the impression you were gonna say more."

"I'm not sure," Fred stumbled for words. "Bill told me got a call from one of the soldiers who delivered the KIA news, asking how they were doing."

Gabriel looked at Hewson and then at Allan.

"Is that normal?" Fred continued. "Does the DOD make calls after notification of next of kin? Bill said the call was polite enough. It was from a career officer who has a daughter who's a medic and in action."

Gabriel handed Fred the letter. "What does this mean?" he asked after reading it.

"It means that either our fallen friends have found the most caring soldiers in the Army, or what's going on has attracted a lot of attention."

"But why?"

Gabriel gave Fred the description of Jenny that Allan had provided. "Is that what Jenny looked like?" Gabriel asked.

"Yes," Fred said, adding some small details. "Is Jenny showing up with the others?"

Gabriel told him it was all speculation, but that the description might help the families, and maybe they'd let him know. He also shared his suspicion that whatever was going on seemed to have a connection to the ward.

He broke off abruptly as Nancy Savard walked into the room, heading directly toward them. The chaplain was not with her. She stopped at Gabriel's bed. "Let's get those bandages changed and then get you down to rehab to work those legs."

"Am I scheduled for therapy today?"

"Not sure, but it can't hurt," Nancy said.

Hewson glanced at Allan and walked back to his bed.

While Nancy changed Gordon's bandages, a nurse and orderly entered the ward and went to Stiles' bed. The orderly carried a bag which he placed next to the lieutenant, who opened it and poked through the contents, taking out some clothes. The nurse had some charts and folders and went through them with the lieutenant. After the paperwork was done, she checked the his bandages and gave him a quick physical once-over—listening to his heart, looking in his eyes and ears, and checking his blood pressure, all of which she noted on the charts.

A doctor came in, looked at the same charts the nurse, and then did the same exam. He spoke for a few moments with the lieutenant, shook his hand and then left. As the doctor was leaving, the orderly returned with a wheelchair.

"Leaving so soon?" Allan called.

"And in style."

"Safe travels," Gabriel said.

The lieutenant got out of bed and began changing into a uniform with the help of the nurse and orderly. After so long in hospital gowns, he seemed oddly different. Hewson whistled.

"Look me up when you guys get back," Stiles said as he was taken out of the ward, raising one hand in farewell.

The ward immediately felt empty even as if there was a hole to be filled, a missing piece of their puzzle.

"Seems odd without him," Gabriel said to Nancy.

"I'm sure you'll get used to it, or someone will take his place," she responded.

"Well, that's the Army," he said. "No matter where you are, people keep moving." She turned away, promising, "I'll be back."

Fred walked over to Gabriel and pointed to the letter. "Not sure what's going on," he said. "Probably nothing."

"The same nothing is happening to a lot of people," Gabriel commented.

"Sometimes it's better to let nothing just happen." Fred advised.

"Maybe," Gabriel responded, "but it don't hurt to check things out."

Nancy came back with a wheelchair. She walked quickly to the sergeant's bed, pulling it alongside and positioning it so Gabriel could lower himself using the overhead frame.

"Same model as the lieutenant's?" Gabriel asked.

"This one doesn't have the same power," she joked and started pushing him down the center aisle making a left once they reached the outside corridor.

"I thought rehab was the other way," Gabriel said.

"I need to go by my office," she explained, wheeling him past the nurses' station and into the darkened corridor that led to her office. They both saw two figures in full dress uniform at the far end.

"Is that Chaplain Jesus down there with someone else?" Gabriel asked. "Never saw him in full dress before."

"I don't know who they are," she told him. "They've been in this corridor for a few days, and you're the only other person who seems to see them."

"The chaplain can't see them?"

"Don't think so. At least, he hasn't said anything."

Nancy wheeled him into her office and, after positioning Gabriel alongside her desk, sat behind it, leaning back in the chair and staring at the door and the figures walking outside. Gabriel studied their faces as they passed the window until he was convinced they were no one he knew.

"Sergeant," she started, "I didn't take you out of the ward for rehab. I saw you slide a letter under your pillow earlier. Is that something you want to share?"

"Just a letter," he stated.

"I've told you all I know about this. And if you know more, I'd like to hear it."

"Why?"

"I understand why you're suspicious. I'm suspicious, too. Chaplain Kirkland is no help. He won't even admit to what he's seen and won't give me a straight answer as to why he's here and what he's doing," Nancy offered.

"Still, I don't see any reason to discuss 'ghost stories' any further."

"What if they're more than ghost stories?"

"What do you mean?"

"What if there's some kind of connection between these deaths? What if the connections go beyond the war?"

"Connections? I know there are all sorts of reports of experiences where loved ones reach out for contact before crossing over, but how could the connections be any further than that?"

"We don't know," she said. "But we can collect information and try to make those connections."

Gabriel wasn't sure what to do. Nancy seemed legitimately concerned that there could be something going on. But what if she was reporting to someone else?

"I got another letter from Cindy Johnson," he finally confessed. "She said that three other people have had five soldiers, including their deceased loved one, visit them."

"Five?"

Gabriel nodded and continued. "It appears that Roy Johnson and Joe Williams, the men who died trying to save me, are with Steve McCafferty and Cliff Craft. The fifth soldier is a woman. I'm writing to Cindy Johnson with a description of Jenny Farmer, the medic who died trying to save Allan."

"Why do you think it's Jenny?"

"I'm taking a stab that there's a connection with everyone in the ward."

"Why was Fred Kidder in the ward?"

"He just happened to come in. So, while he was there, since he knew Jenny in high school, I asked him to confirm the description. I don't know if there's more of a connection than that."

"Interesting. Anything else?"

Gabriel grew quiet, wondering how much he should tell. He really wanted to trust someone. "Okay, so I really don't know who to trust here."

"Well, take a chance with me," she said.

He shared with her the information he'd gotten from Cindy, along with his reservations.

"How is that suspicious?" she asked. "Seems like a thoughtful and nice thing to do."

"Jane Craft, John McCafferty, and Dave Williams all received similar follow-up calls at about the same time."

"Maybe it's new DOD policy," she suggested. "The Army *is* PR conscious."

"Maybe. But the calls all had at least one question about whether they'd seen the deceased more than once."

"How did the callers know about the loved ones seeing the deceased?"

"I don't know, unless they were told at the time of notification."

"And you think all these calls are connected?"

"They all leave the same contact number."

"Even that means nothing."

"Well, and I've got nothing but time," Gabriel said, "so I might as well follow it up."

"Why are they here?" Nancy said, looking at the soldiers in front of her office.

"I don't know."

"Mind if I see that letter?"

"I'll slip it to you when we get back to my bed."

She wheeled him through the doors to her office. The two soldiers were making their turn at the far end of the corridor. Kirkland walked through the double doors.

"Thought you were taking him to rehab?"

"I needed to pick something up. We're heading there now," she said, walking past him without looking at him.

"How are you doing, Sergeant?" Kirkland asked.

"Better every day."

"Seeing any more ghosts?"

"More every day" Gabriel said, very seriously.

The three of them walked to the rehab center.

"Lance," Nancy said, "there's really no need for you to be here. This is something that lowly nurses and orderlies do."

"I never know where I'll find inspiration for a future sermon," he answered.

"You haven't given a sermon in years," Nancy said, agitated. Gabriel was surprised at how angry she sounded.

"What do you say, Sergeant?" Kirkland addressed him. "Can I hang around?"

"Word is that Nancy and I need a chaperone," he quipped, breaking the tension.

"So, what did you pick up at your office, more of those letters?" Lance asked Nancy once Gabriel had started his exercises.

"Lance, in case you don't realize it, I outrank you." Nancy's psychology degree gave her the rank of Lieutenant Commander while the chaplain was a captain.

"Meaning?"

"I have no need, nor am I compelled, to answer your questions," she said.

"I know you have some letters," he insisted.

"Lance, I will report you."

"I may report *you*, Nancy."

"What are you doing here?" She turned to him. "When I called you, I thought you'd be able to offer some help, but you're not. By doing nothing, you're just a distraction. Why do you stay?"

"I report to Commander Donner and no one else."

"You need to stay away from my patients."

"Why, Nancy? What are you hiding?"

"I am not hiding anything," she said stiffly. "You just don't believe your own eyes."

"Nancy, I want to know what you know."

"Your mind is shut, Lance," she said flatly, going to Gabriel, who was just finishing the exercises.

"You two make quite a couple," Gabriel said sarcastically.

"It goes back a long way," Nancy said as Lance left the room.

"Leaving, huh?" Gabriel said. "Well, with the way you were bickering, that's probably a good thing."

She wheeled him back to the ward where he lifted himself off the chair with the help of the overhead frame and took the two steps to the bed. As he was positioning himself, he slipped his hand under the pillow and pulled out the latest letter, only hesitating slightly before handing it to her. She promised she'd return it, along with the others he'd shared, gave him a thin smile, and left him with orders to get some rest. As soon as she was out of sight, Gabriel started writing to Cindy Johnson.

TWENTY-NINE

Lieutenant Maureen O'Grady stared at the order on the desk in front of her; she couldn't believe it. Why would the Army want to contact someone again and re-interview someone who was coping with such devastating news? She'd had the order for four days and just could not bring herself to make the call.

She was one of a half dozen women officers assigned to the DOD to deliver news to next of kin. She mostly rode with a male counterpart and he gave the news to the families of male KIA. She and the five other women were the ones who delivered the news of women killed in the line of duty. She felt it an honor to do this.

Beyond the military dress, her appearance was always impeccable: soft complexion, blue eyes, very little makeup, her light red hair pulled back but not tight—just enough to show military respect but also convey openness to people in a desperate moment. Her voice was very soothing. As an added bonus, she could do what the men could not and actually physically comfort and console the families. Many, many times she'd held the father of a female killed in action as he sobbed, weakened by the terrible news.

She'd kept in contact with many of what she thought of as 'her' families after the notifications and was almost always asked to attend the funeral. She'd become very close with some of them, accepting their calls, feeling as though they might view her as their final contact to the deceased. But this was the first time the Army had ordered her to interview a family again. She considered it more than an intrusion, and didn't know how to deal with it.

She'd felt an immediate connection to the Farmer family, perhaps because of her own closeness to her father. She remembered Bill Farmer after she delivered the news: he was shocked, devastated, shattered—and swearing he'd just seen his daughter in full dress uniform, adamant he had just held her in his arms.

She'd watched as both he and the little boy searched for Jenny. It was only when he was handed the envelope containing Jenny's personal things that he accepted the truth. She'd caught him as he doubled over in emotional agony. Remembering his sobs brought tears to her own eyes.

"Women aren't supposed to be in war," she remembered Bill crying out, "let alone die in war. What have we come to?"

"I'll sit with you for a while," she said to Bill. "I've got time."

They'd talked a few times since, like old friends. Now that closeness was making this order almost impossible to follow. She didn't know if she could make the call. She felt that not only was the DOD intruding on a family who had given the ultimate, but they were now intruding in her own life. But if she didn't do it soon, there'd be hell to pay because her report had not been submitted. She felt sick to her stomach as she dialed.

"Bill?" Maureen said as he picked up the phone.

"Hi, Mo. Nice of you to call," Bill said.

"Well, this time, I'm also checking in for the Army," she explained.

"The Army?"

"Yep, I'm supposed to call you. This is the first time I've ever been asked to make a follow-up contact."

"Well, you know how we are, Mo," he said. "We miss Jenny very much. It's so hard." His voice trailed off as it started to crack. Maureen felt her eyes start to fill.

"I know, Bill. It is hard," she repeated and then continued. "That day I gave you the news and you said that Jenny was just there, you even went looking for her."

"That's right," he said. "You were so understanding."

"Bill," Maureen said. "I know this is a tough question, but have you seen Jenny since?"

He was very quiet, and Maureen could almost feel him thinking. "Mo, are you asking this, or is the Army?"

"The Army, Bill. I would never intrude."

"I wish it were you, Mo. I've given—we've given—enough. I refuse to give an answer to that question."

"Thank you, Bill, for your understanding. That wasn't easy for me to ask."

Bill was quiet for a long time. She couldn't tell what emotion he was trying to control, anger or grief.

"Why would the Army be interested in this?" he finally asked. "Why would they ask these questions? What could they gain from it?"

Maureen said, " I honestly don't know. When I got the order, I looked at it, buried it, and waited until I knew I had to do what it said and ask you that question. I have no idea why they want to know."

"So, off the record?" Bill asked.

"Okay, but you don't have to do this."

"We have seen her twice since you gave us the news. Once she was by herself, standing in the front yard."

"And the second time?"

"That one was odd," he said in a weak voice.

"Odder than seeing Jenny?"

"She was standing in the front yard with four other soldiers."

"Four others. She wasn't alone?"

"I was in the front room reading and looked out the window and saw someone in uniform coming up the road, too far away for me to recognize."

"But isn't that the way she came before?"

"Yes, but this time was different. There was a second soldier behind the first, then a third. In all, there were five of them walking in single file, all in perfect step and all in full dress. They walked up the road, turned into the driveway, and then stood in front of the house."

"What did you do?" Maureen asked.

"I couldn't do anything at first, I was just too surprised. I just watched them. Then I went to the front door."

"Did she say anything to you?"

"No, Mo," Bill said, his voice cracking. "She had the most peaceful expression, but she just looked at me. I opened the door and went out. I asked her — I'm sorry, Mo — I was crying. I asked her what she wanted."

"Please, take your time."

"She never answered me. She seemed to be sad that I was crying. Then, one by one, they just turned and walked away. Jenny was the last one to leave."

Maureen didn't know what to make of what he told her. Maybe she could ask around, see if anyone else was being asked to re-interview people. Maybe she could find out the reason for the interviews.

"Bill, I promise I won't tell your story to anyone," she said before hanging up.

Then she sat looking at the comments section of the report for a long moment, before filling it in by writing that Bill had not seen Jenny since the day of notification. If she stated that Bill had refused to answer, it would mean another call, maybe from someone who did not know the situation.

While she had been on the phone, a KIA notification was placed in her box. She was to meet with Lt. Vincent Russo to deliver the notification to the next of kin of Kimberly Fisher.

Corporal Fisher was KIA during a rocket attack on the base where she was stationed. Kimberly was a computer tech, one of the specialists that should never see action, let alone get wounded. Maureen thought it would be tough for a computer tech to even get a paper cut. Maureen realized that, since this case involved a woman, she would have to take the lead, with Russo accompanying her as backup. The order said to meet him late in the afternoon. It would be the last assignment of the day and might mean a long night, depending on how well the next of kin handled the news. She straightened up her desk and then walked to the meeting room to wait for Russo.

The room was empty and clean, with two long tables placed end to end and gray folding chairs pushed up against them. The fluorescent lights overhead were in one long row that ran the length of the room, directly over the tables. Maureen sat at one end of the tables, facing the wooden podium that stood at the opposite end.

A tall officer, thin with short dark hair, walked in the room. He was young looking, which surprised Maureen. In her experience, older personnel were selected for this duty.

"Lieutenant O'Grady?" the young officer asked.

"Lieutenant Russo?" she responded.

He approached and held out his hand. "Lieutenant Vincent Russo."

"Maureen O'Grady." She stood and shook his hand.

There was an awkward silence before he spoke. "I've never given notification," he said sheepishly, "on a woman KIA."

"Don't worry. I'll take the lead," she said.

"Call me Vinnie," he said. "And thank you. I really don't know what I'd say or how emotional it would come out."

Maureen nodded her understanding. "I'm not sure what's worse, dying in combat or giving the news," she said quietly.

Maureen liked Russo immediately. He was military, but she sensed a special understanding in him. "We should go," she said.

The drive to the Fisher's home took just under an hour. They spoke lightly of their time in the Army. Neither of them had seen combat but both had friends who were KIA.

"When we're about two blocks away, pull over. I'll need to take a few moments," Maureen said, and Vinnie nodded.

When they were close, he stopped the car on the side of the road. Maureen opened the letter and slowly read again how Kimberly Fisher died. She put the information back into the envelope and then closed her eyes. Bowing her head and breathing deeply, she brought her hands together in prayer. Seeing this, Russo also lowered his head. They sat quietly for a couple of minutes.

"Okay," she said, touching him on the back of his hand.

"It's around this corner." He pointed to his left. "Third house on the right."

After making the turn, they counted the houses on the street. At the third house, they saw three figures standing in the front yard. A man and a woman had their arms around a soldier.

"Are you sure this is the right house?" Maureen asked.

Russo pulled out the directions and re-read them, checking the number and looking back over his shoulder at the street sign. "This is the street and number on the form," he said.

They passed the house. Both the man and the woman looked at them as they drove by.

Russo made a U turn at the end of the street, then slowly drove back up and came to a stop in front of the house. The man and woman stepped away from the soldier and walked toward them. Maureen and Vinnie got out of the car, pulled their uniforms straight and moved toward the approaching couple. The soldier turned to face them, and Maureen saw it was a woman. She stopped in her tracks.

"We may be lost," Russo said softly. "We are looking for the Fisher residence." He read off the address.

"That is this address. How can we help you officers?" the man asked, with the woman standing close to him. Maureen looked behind them. The young female soldier was no longer there. "Where'd the soldier go?"

149

she whispered to Vinnie.

"I don't know," he answered.

"Are you Harold and Helen Fisher?" Maureen asked seriously.

"Yes," he responded as Helen nodded.

"Is your daughter, Kimberly Fisher, a corporal in the U.S. Army?"

"Yes. Do you know Kimberly? She's right here," Harold said, turning around. "Where'd she go, Helen? Maybe she went inside. Could you go get her?" He took a step toward the two officers, offering his hand in greeting. "She just came up the walkway," Harold said. "We were so surprised. In her last e-mail she told us she probably wouldn't get home for another year, and yet here she is."

Maureen looked at him, not knowing what to say.

Helen came out from the house. "She's not in there, Harry."

"Well, maybe she went around the back," Harold said, walking around the side of the house.

"What are we witnessing?" Vinnie asked Maureen, who had no answer.

Harold returned, looking confused. He crossed the lawn and looked up and down the street. "Let me check the house," he said.

"Mr. Fisher," Maureen said softly.

"Just a minute," Harold insisted and quickly went into the house. They could hear him calling his daughter's name, his voice sounding sadder and more urgent each time. Helen stood quietly, her face growing pale. Harold came out and sat on the front steps. His wife moved next to him. She leaned her head on his shoulder and entwined her arm in his until they grasped hands.

"Mr. and Mrs. Fisher." Maureen walked toward them.

"Please don't," Harold begged, choking on the words. Helen buried her face in his shoulder. Maureen walked slowly, trying not to intrude, knowing these last few seconds were the only thing left of the world as they knew it.

"I am Maureen O'Grady and this is Vincent Russo. This is very difficult. We regret to inform you that your daughter, Kimberly Fisher, has been killed in the line of duty in service to our country."

Both parents sobbed, shoulders convulsing. Helen took a deep, rasping breath. "She was right here," she said. "We were just holding her.

My baby ... my wonderful Kimmie. It can't be true."

"You drove past us, didn't you see her?" Harold asked.

"We know how difficult this is," Vinnie said. He moved his hand to his face, pretending to scratch his cheek but really wiping away a tear.

"Didn't you see her?" Harold asked again. "All three of us were hugging each other while you drove by the first time," he said, pointing to a spot on the front lawn.

A man walked across the street. "Harry, Helen, is everything all right?"

Helen stood and practically ran inside.

"Jim, Jim," Harold said, crying uncontrollably, "We've lost Kimmie. She was killed in action."

"Killed?" Jim asked. "Harry, how could that be? Didn't I just see her? I thought it was Kimmie come home. It was the three of you on the lawn."

"You saw her, Jim?" Harold asked.

"I thought it was her."

"Please Jim, check the street," Harold begged. "Find her for me."

"Mr. Fisher," Maureen said.

"Why didn't you see her? Jim did."

"Mr. Fisher, things like this are terrible. There are no words." Maureen could hear Helen sobbing inside. "Would you mind if I go inside to help your wife?"

"No, sure...please," Harold said. Maureen started up the steps and looked back at Vinnie who was already bending down to attempt to comfort Harold Fisher.

The woman who lived next door came running into the yard. "Harry? What is it?"

"Joan, these officers are here to give us the news that Kimmie is dead, killed in action."

"How is that possible?" Joan asked. "She was a computer tech; she was never near guns."

"That's right. That's right," Harold said. "She wasn't a combat soldier, so how could she be killed?" He sounded angry.

"It was a rocket attack," Russo said quietly, knowing there was no gentle way to say those words.

"Oh, God,"

"Did you see her Joan?" Harold asked. "Jim did."

"No, Harry, I didn't." Joan looked at him, bewildered.

Jim returned from his search to announce, "I can't find her, Harry."

Russo opened the envelope attached to the notification and handed it to Harold, who poured out the contents. A necklace slid out.

Maureen came out of the house with Helen clinging to her arm.

"That's her necklace," Helen cried. "It's true, Harry. It's true. We've lost our Kimmie."

Still more neighbors arrived. Maureen and Vinnie helped the grieving couple into the house and most of the neighbors followed.

"This is what we have," Maureen said, passing them a sheet of paper. "It gives some details on what happened and when she will be home."

"Thank you, officers," Harold said.

"Please call me Maureen. Here's my work number if you need anything." She thought for a moment. "And here's my home number. Please let me know if I can do anything to help."

"Did you know Kimmie?" Helen asked.

"No, ma'am." Maureen looked around the room. "But judging by the support you have here, it's obvious she was something special."

"Are you leaving?" Harold asked.

"We can stay as long as you want," Russo responded. Maureen nodded.

A short while later, feeling they had done all that they could, and knowing that the remembrances the Fishers were sharing with their neighbors would bring them some small comfort, the pair took their leave.

Once back in the car, Maureen said, "What did we just see?"

"A ghost?" Vinnie answered.

They rode in silence, each convinced they'd seen a female soldier standing in front of the house with Harold and Helen Fisher.

"Have you ever heard of anything like that?" Vinnie broke the silence. Maureen was quiet. "I've heard stories," he continued, "but never witnessed it."

"Stories?"

Vinnie related what had happened on the day he delivered the news about her husband's death to Cindy Johnson, that both she and her child were convinced that Roy was there.

"I had a similar situation with Jenny Farmer," Maureen told him. "Both father and daughter said they'd had ridden home with Jenny from the park."

"Okay." Russo took a deep breath. "I recently spoke with Mrs. Johnson. She told me she saw her husband again after the notification. Not only did she him again the day hisbody arrived, but the chaplain and the base commander saw him also."

"You interviewed her?"

"Yeah, some kind of crappy order coming from someone pretty high up. Why?"

"I got the same kind of order. I had to interview Jenny Farmer's father and asked him if he'd seen her again."

"And?"

"Officially, he told me no. He said they had given enough," Maureen said.

"And?"

"Off the record, he said he's seen her twice more, once alone and the last time with four other soldiers."

"Four other dead soldiers?"

"That would be my guess," Maureen responded. "I don't know where to go with this, who to ask, but I want to know more," Maureen said.

"Who do we ask? Should we be obvious?"

"I'll ask a few careful question of my boss, like why an interview and why only some. Is there a connection between the families being re-interviewed? I want to see what he says."

"Maybe you'll get a better answer than I did," Russo stated.

THIRTY

Cindy Johnson opened the letter from Gabriel Gordon. It was a little more battered than usual.

"Looks like it walked and swam its way from Germany," she said out loud.

In the letter, he told her what was going on in the ward and what he thought might be the connection between the soldiers in his ward and the soldiers people were seeing back home in the States. He explained about Allan, who had been seriously burned in the war, and how a female medic named Jenny Farmer died trying to help him. The letter included a description of Jenny, right down to the ribbons and medals she wore, the color of her eyes and hair, complexion, height, and even freckles.

Cindy stopped reading, realizing that description matched the woman who came with Roy and the three other soldiers. *All five of these soldiers are connected to one ward in Germany? Why? Is the U.S. military keeping those men in that one ward because of ghost stories?*

Gabriel went on to say that he was confiding in a nurse named Nancy Savard, who was interested in these situations. He also said that Chaplain Kirkland was in Germany and that he believed that Kirkland was the same chaplain who saw Roy when she asked to view the body. Kirkland, or "Chaplain Jesus," as Gabriel called him, was not as open as the nurse was, so he wasn't someone Gabriel confided in. He didn't think Nurse Savard did, either. He ended the letter asking to be included in any new information.

Cindy picked up the phone and thought for a second before dialing Dave Williams' number. Dave was the first person outside of the military she talked to about Roy and what she was seeing. He seemed understanding and sympathetic, and believed something was going on.

"Dave? This is Cindy Johnson."

"Hi, Cindy. So you must have more information?"

She read him the letter from Gabriel Gordon, again explaining he was the sergeant that Roy and Joe were trying to help when they were killed. She then reviewed the details of Hewson's injuries and experiences, including Craft and McCafferty.

"It seems confirmed that these four soldiers are together when we see them, but where does the female soldier come in?" Dave asked.

"There's another wounded soldier in the German ward," Cindy said "named Allan. He was severely burned." Cindy went on to explain how Jenny Farmer was killed trying to help Allan after the attack on the Humvee. She read the Jenny Farmer description.

Dave responded by telling Cindy the description matched the woman who was outside his bar with the other soldiers. "Right down to the freckles." He was quiet for a long moment before asking, "What's going on, Cindy?"

"I don't know," she responded, not trying to hide the emotion in her voice. "Why won't they stay at rest? What are they trying to tell us, and what is the connection with the ward?"

"Cindy, Joe is outside," Dave whispered. "Cindy—"

She didn't want to answer. She didn't want to look outside her own house. She didn't want to see any more of this.

"Is he by himself?" she finally asked.

"No, there are four others with him and one of them is Jenny Farmer. Are they outside your place?

"I don't know," she responded in a whisper.

"Can't you see?"

"No."

"Cindy, are you looking?"

"I don't want to." She was sitting at the table, her back to the front room, looking straight down.

"Please, Cindy."

She got up from her chair and walked through the front room, glancing at the window in the corner, seeing a uniformed man standing and looking at the house. She took short, deep breaths as she continued walking to the larger window in the front room. She stared at six soldiers, standing and looking at her home.

"Dave," she said, "Roy is here with five other soldiers. I have a total of six here, Dave."

"There are six here, too, Cindy," Dave said, in barely a whisper. "Another female soldier just showed up. My God, what's going on?"

"Mommy, why is Daddy standing there with those Army men?" Dave heard Cindy's daughter Carol ask.

"I don't know, honey," Cindy responded.

"Isn't Daddy with God?"

Tears ran from Dave's eyes. He could feel the ache Cindy must be going through hearing a question like that.

"Yes, Carol, Daddy is with God and so are those other soldiers."

"Then why are they here?"

"Cindy," Dave asked gently, "should we ask?"

"I can't, Dave," Cindy said. "Carol, please stay in the house."

"But it's Daddy!" Dave heard the child and a door open. "Hi, Daddy!"

Roy Johnson smiled widely at his daughter

"Carol," Cindy called, as she came to the door. "Please come in." She pulled the little girl back. "Roy," Cindy continued, "why... what is going on... why are you all here?"

Roy smiled understandingly at his wife. The smile relaxed her.

"Dave," Cindy said. "Can you talk with Joe?"

Dave put the phone down, and she heard the door open.

"Joe?" Dave said. "What are you doing here? Why are you and these other soldiers here?" Dave got back on the phone. "Cindy, he didn't answer me. He just smiled."

"That's what I got from Roy," she said. "Hold on, I've got another call." She switched the phone. "Hello?"

"Mrs. Johnson, this is John McCafferty. Steve is here!" The old man started talking as she picked up the phone.

"Mr. McCafferty, Roy is here with five other soldiers. So I have a total of six now."

"There are five others with Steve, too. What's going on?"

"I'm not sure. Hold on a second, okay?" She switched back to Dave.

"Cindy, I have six in front of my tavern, and people are beginning to gather."

"Other people are seeing them?"

"Yes, even traffic on the street is beginning to slow."

"Hold on, Dave." She switched to John McCafferty. "Dave Williams has the six soldiers in front of his tavern in Seattle. But now others, people on the street, are seeing them."

"What? Strangers are seeing these men?"

"Can I call you back, John?" she asked.

"Of course," he said.

She changed the phone back to Dave and immediately heard the note of another call coming in. "Dave, sorry, another call."

Dave told her to take it, and that he'd try to call her later.

"Cindy, this is Jane Craft," she heard as soon as she switched to the incoming call.

"Clifford is there?"

Jane's voice sounded weak, exhausted, with no strength to it. She'd never sounded strong in the few times that they'd talked, but it was the slightest voice Cindy had ever heard. She strained to hear the woman explain that Clifford and now five other soldiers were standing in front of the house, and two of the other soldiers were women.

"Two are women," Cindy repeated.

"Yes, they are at your place, too?"

Cindy confirmed she was seeing the same thing as Jane. She then told her about Dave and John, both with six soldiers and two women among the six.

Jane responded with a sigh. "Cindy, do you know what is going on?"

"Jane," Cindy said, hating to ask, "Can you talk to Clifford?"

"I couldn't," the woman started to weep uncontrollably.

THIRTY-ONE

Dave Williams looked out the tavern window at the soldiers standing shoulder to shoulder in a straight line and staring back at him. Joe was the hardest to ignore; he had a slight smile on his face, one Dave had seen millions of times growing up, but it seemed a bit more peaceful now. Crowds gathered on the sidewalk at both ends of where the soldiers stood. The traffic was almost at standstill, with people getting out of their cars to look at the soldiers before moving on again.

Dave opened the door and stepped outside, walking slowly over to his brother. It was as if all the normal sounds of the city had stopped; it was more than quiet. Joe watched him coming. People continued to stare at the six soldiers in full dress uniform in front of a tavern in the middle of the day.

"Why, Joe?" Dave said to his brother, whispering close to his brother's ear. "Why are you here?"

Joe responded with a reassuring smile.

"Why are you all here?" Dave said a little louder to the other five soldiers standing with his brother. They responded with smiles.

Dave looked back to Joe, but said nothing. He reached out, touching his brother's chin and letting his hand run down across the ribbons and medals on his chest. He looked into his brother's eyes once again. Then, putting both hands on Joe's shoulders, he drew his into an embrace. Abruptly, the silence was shattered by the sound of police sirens. Joe broke the embrace and stood tall and straight.

The street outside the tavern was so choked with cars that the police had to park at each end of the block. They pushed their way on foot, stopping suddenly when they saw the six soldiers standing at attention. A few people with cell phones and cameras started taking pictures.

Without any discernible signal, the soldiers turned as one, walking away in step, as the police and crowds gave way so they could pass. Light applause swelled to cheers and supportive shouts as the soldiers walked down the street and turned the corner. Some children ran after them and quickly returned, shouting, "They're gone! We don't know where they went."

One of the police officers, Kenny McGuire, walked up to Dave. Kenny was an average size young man who'd only been on the force a few years. He was also a regular at Dave's tavern.

"Dave?" Kenny whispered. "That looked like Joe! Was it Joe?"

Dave's eyes filled quickly. He wiped away a tear and nodded.

"Jesus Christ, Dave" Kenny said. "Joe's dead, KIA. What is going on?"

THIRTY-TWO

Maureen O'Grady poured water into the kettle, and then placed it on the stove for tea; the TV was on in the background in her small apartment. She was feeling emotionally drained by the experience at the Fisher home. She was positive that both she and Russo had seen the female soldier on the Fishers' front lawn. The Fishers swore that their daughter had been there. Neighbors had seen her. *What in hell was going on?*

The water came to a boil. Maureen filled the cup, walked to the living room, and sat on the couch, barely following the news highlighting the down economy and other local issues. The report switched to a view of a different city; the words scrolling across the bottom of the screen identified it as Seattle. It was a grainy, still picture of six soldiers in full dress uniform standing shoulder to shoulder at attention in front of a tavern.

Maureen watched the entire report, leaning forward as if trying to get as close to Seattle as possible. When she heard the name 'Joe Williams' she thought the name sounded very familiar. Was that one of the names Russo had mentioned? Where had she heard it before? Her phone rang.

"Hello?"

"Maureen, this is Harold Fisher."

"Mr. Fisher, how are you? Is everything okay?"

"Maureen, we just had a visit from six soldiers who stood on our front lawn, looking at the house. The neighbors with us in the house and up and down the street saw them, too."

"Six soldiers," Maureen said cautiously. "Did they say why they were there?" She was thinking about the news report she'd just watched.

"They said nothing. Helen saw them first and walked out to the porch. She originally thought it might have been a visit showing respect for Kimberly, but…"

Maureen, sensing the man's emotion, stayed quiet, waiting for him to catch his breath and continue.

"Kimmie was there, smiling at us."

Maureen couldn't believe what she was hearing and didn't know what to say.

"Kimberly was there." Maureen said.

"Yes, I walked out and found Helen on her knees, crying and asking Kimmie what she wanted. Kimmie smiled—so peacefully so understanding, so at peace."

"Did she say anything?"

"No. But, when I broke down, I put my hands out to her and we hugged." His voice broke, and he was silent for several moments.

"Maureen," he finally said, after he composed himself. "What is going on? We just saw a report from Seattle about six soldiers in front of a tavern. Kimmie was with those soldiers. Can you tell us what is going on?"

"I don't know, Mr. Fisher. I really don't."

Maureen spent a few moments calming the Fishers, telling Harold she'd call if she found out any information.

Staring out the window, she thought, these are more than ghost stories. People other than family are seeing these dead soldiers. But who else should she or could she call? Her phone rang again.

"What is going on?" Vinnie Russo asked, without even identifying himself. "Did you see the report from Seattle?"

"Yes."

"I got a call from Cindy Johnson," he said. "She said that Roy Johnson, her husband, was standing outside her house and also outside the tavern. He was among the same six soldiers in both places."

"Roy Johnson and Joe William together in both places?" Maureen said, remembering where she'd heard the name.

"Cindy was talking to Joe's brother, Dave, when it happened, so she knew Joe was there. She also called John McCafferty, the grandfather of one of the other soldiers who is showing up with the others."

Maureen told him about the call she had just received from Harold Fisher. She then told Russo she was going to call Jenny Farmer's dad.

Maureen knew immediately from Bill Farmer's voice that he had seen Jenny.

"Bill," she said as he picked up the phone, "this is—"

"Mo," Bill said, the emotion in his voice easy to hear. "My God, what is going on? Jenny was here with five other soldiers and there was another woman with them. Four men and two women, including Jenny."

"When?"

"At the same time the same six soldiers were standing outside that bar in Seattle."

"Were you able to speak to Jenny?" Maureen asked softly.

"I tried," Bill explained. "I asked why she was back, what was going on. She didn't answer. She just smiled and hugged me. Jesus Christ, Mo, what is this?"

Maureen tried to be comforting. She told Bill Farmer the same things she'd told Harold Fisher, including that she'd get back to him if she found out anything.

They hung up and she dialed Russo. "We need to talk to Jacobs; something is going on."

"You think Jacobs knows anything?" Russo asked.

"You think they'll let us talk with Rogers or General Lent?" Maureen said quickly.

"No. I guess we start with Jacobs."

THIRTY-THREE

Gabriel Gordon, James Hewson, and Allan Paul watched the Seattle news report from the rec room in the hospital.

"That's Roy Johnson and Joe Williams." Gordon pointed to two of the soldiers in the line "You guys recognize anyone?"

"McCafferty and Craft," Hewson said.

"Jenny Farmer," Allan added.

"The other is Kimberly Fisher." A whisper came from behind them.

"Who?" Hewson asked.

"Kimberly Fisher." A stocky Marine, with almost-shaved blond hair, pushed himself toward them in a wheelchair. His legs were gone, and there was a fresh scar on his check. "I'm Greg Adams," he said. "I was in the building when Kimberly died in the rocket attack." He slapped his thighs. "They say I'm the lucky one." His blue eyes flashed as he was talking.

"How long you been here?" Gordon asked.

"Since yesterday. Seems they decided to put me in with you guys just a few minutes ago." They all turned back to the TV, watching an interview with a woman who lived near the tavern and saying that it was Joe Williams standing in front of it.

The TV went off. There was still power to the rest of the room but the TV remained dark. Hewson looked over to one of the orderlies. "Hey, TV?" Hewson said.

The orderly was already trying to figure out what happened. "There's power to it," the orderly said.

"Try another channel," Allan suggested.

The orderly pointed the remote toward the TV and an old rerun of *All in the Family* came on the screen. The orderly changed back to the original channel and all it showed was a black screen. No static, no test pattern— just black.

"Must be something going on with the TV station," the orderly said.

"See if you can find another station with the news," Gabriel asked. The orderly flipped through the channels but no other station was broadcasting news at that time. The TV settled back on *All in the Family*.

"The one station that's broadcasting news about servicemen is the one that's having technical difficulties?" Greg Adams shrugged his shoulders while looking at the others.

Nancy Savard and Lance Kirkland walked into the rec room. Nancy was walking slightly in front of the chaplain, almost as if she was trying to get away from him. She was not smiling.

"Looks like you three have met your new roommate," she said.

"Greg?" Hewson said. "No need for us to meet. We're old friends; probably went to different schools together."

No one laughed.

"We were just watching the news," Gabriel said. "We saw a report about some soldiers standing in front of a bar in Seattle." He was looking directly at Nancy. "Funny, that's now the only TV station we can't get."

"Technical difficulties always seem to hit at inconvenient times," Kirkland responded.

Gabriel watched Nancy. Her expression never changed; it was straight faced and serious when she walked into the room, and it was straight faced and serious now.

"We need to talk with you individually," she told them, as two other officers walked up. "So, to get this done quickly as possible, we're each going to chat with one of you."

Gabriel and I will talk." Kirkland walked forward. The two other officers took Hewson and Allan.

"Looks like I get you, Greg," Nancy said.

Kirkland wheeled Gabriel out of the room and into a small sitting area a short distance from the nurse's station.

"Sergeant," Kirkland said stiffly, "you've been writing to Cindy Johnson."

"Is that against the Geneva Convention?" Gabriel asked. "In case you're not aware, her husband died trying to save me."

"We don't need the sarcasm, Sergeant."

"Well, then, I'm at a loss as to what we do need, Captain," Gabriel said, staring directly into the chaplain's eyes.

"Are you talking to Mrs. Johnson about her thinking that she's been seeing her husband?"

"It comes up in passing. Are you talking with her about what you *have* seen?"

"Why?"

"Why what?" Gabriel was enjoying this discussion.

"Why would you want to add to the woman's grief?"

"Add to her grief? Look, Chaplain Jesus, I know you saw Roy Johnson in that hangar. Don't you think you could soothe that woman's grief by admitting to it? Or are you upset that it was not your doing that raised this dead?"

"You know, Sergeant, I have to write a report about our conversation. How would it look on your record to have it down that you were uncooperative?"

"Uncooperative?" Gabriel yelled. The nurses stopped and looked at them, and he slapped his legs. "Un-fucking-cooperative?" he said, just as loudly. "I've fucking cooperated enough."

"Yes, Sergeant," Kirkland said, trying to keep his voice down. "Your sacrifice is noted, but talking ghost stories with the family members of those who gave the ultimate cannot help."

"Admit what you saw, Chaplain." Gabriel almost spit the title off his tongue.

"Do not, Sergeant … do not continue writing to Cindy Johnson." Kirkland was angry. Gabriel did not respond.

"Do you understand what I what I just told you?" Kirkland said, sternly.

"No, *Sir*," again letting the name spit off his tongue. "I do not understand."

"You have been given an order, Sergeant!" Kirkland said, even louder.

Nancy walked into the corridor at the end of the conversation. She glared at Kirkland.

"What order is that, *Sir*? That the sergeant cannot correspond with the family of the man who died saving his life?" Gabriel was leaning forward in the wheelchair, directly in the chaplain's face.

"Do not correspond with Mrs. Johnson. Is that clear?" Kirkland repeated.

Gabriel's face turned red. He lifted himself in his wheelchair as small red patches appeared on his bandages where he had slapped his legs earlier.

"No, it is *not* clear," Gabriel screamed.

"Do not write to anyone."

"Fuck you, Captain."

Nancy glared at Kirkland, before turning Gabriel away.

"Captain Kirkland, consider yourself on report, and the report *will* recommend a general court martial. Is *that* clear, Captain?"

Kirkland stood and tried to get in front of her.

"Dismissed, Captain, and leave the hospital. You will be notified as to whom and where you should report," Nancy said, not bothering to try to hide her disgust.

One of the other nurses quietly came over to Gabriel and began to check his bandages.

"I will help him," Nancy said to the nurse. "This patient will be my personal responsibility."

Greg Adams had been waiting at the nurse's station since Nancy and he finished speaking, and so was able to observe the entire interaction unfolding between Gabriel and the chaplain, as well as Nancy's intervention. He watched Kirkland walk quickly past the nurse's station, through the doors and into the corridor that led to Nancy's office.

Nancy glanced at Greg and asked the nurse to move him to the ward. The two wounded men were wheeled in side by side, never looking at each other.

Nancy wheeled Gabriel to his bed. Gabriel waved off her offer for assistance and lifted himself off the chair and into his bed. She looked at his legs.

"Looks like the bleeding is not coming from any place too deep. I'll change the bandages and it should stop quickly," she told him.

Gabriel leaned back, his head on a propped up pillow, his face still red with anger, frustration, and some embarrassment. He didn't look at Nancy. "I was trying so hard to get out of that chair," he told her. "If I had, Chaplain Jesus might have been visiting his loved ones before the DOD delivered KIA notification."

"Kirkland may put you on report, Sergeant," she said seriously.

"I've given enough," he said, tapping his legs.

She whispered in Gabriel's ear.

"Everyone in the States, up to the President, is aware of that news broadcast."

"Why was it cut off?"

"Like I said," She looked him square in the eyes, "Everyone is aware of that broadcast."

Gabriel did not respond.

"Have you heard from Cindy Johnson?" she asked.

"Not since my last letter with the description of Jenny Farmer."

"Might be a good time to find another way for you to contact her. I'm not sure your letters or hers will ever be delivered."

"Is that an order?" Gabriel was still angry.

No, of course not," Nancy said. "But if you actually want to continue communicating, you need to find another way."

Gabriel felt something small against his hip. He reached down and touched a long narrow piece of plastic about the size of a pack of cigarettes, only thinner. He lifted it slightly and looked, seeing a cell phone. When he flipped it open, a piece of paper fell out that had the letters CJ and a phone number written on it.

"Initials," is all Nancy said.

CJ, Gabriel thought. "Cindy Johnson?" he whispered. He was rewarded by the first smile he'd seen from Nancy that afternoon. He immediately started calculating the time difference between Germany and Arizona.

"*We will* talk," Nancy said. She finished changing his bandages and left.

The ward was quiet. Allan and Hewson were not back yet. Greg sat up in bed.

"Chaplain Jesus?" he called out. Both he and Gabriel started laughing. Gabriel maneuvered himself into his wheelchair and scooted down to Greg's bed.

"Let me fill you in on a few things," he told the Marine.

"And now you are here with a story of another fallen soldier, one who's showing up with the others. We think there's a connection," he told Greg in conclusion.

"Sounds that way to me," Greg agreed.

THIRTY-FOUR

The president was in his residence; he had a DVD copy of the Seattle news report on the TV and was watching it for the sixth time. He called down to his secretary.

"Get me the commander of the DOD," he said. In a few seconds, General Fielding Lent was on the line.

"Mr. President," Lent said.

"General, have you seen the news report from Seattle?"

"Yes, sir."

"Well, General, what do you think?" The president often got frustrated when military men only answered the question directly, seemingly out of convenience.

"I don't know what to think, Mr. President. The witness said it was Joe Williams, a soldier killed in action."

"What does the brother say?"

"The brother is not saying anything."

"Who are the other five soldiers?"

"We think they are Roy Williams, Clifford Craft, Steve McCafferty, Jenny Farmer, and Kimberly Fisher," Lent told him.

"All active duty?" the president asked.

"Not anymore, sir."

"What?"

"All KIA," Lent declared.

"General," the president said, trying to control his voice, "Are you confirming that there were six dead soldiers in front of a bar in Seattle?"

"The soldiers fit the descriptions, Mr. President."

"What are you going to do about it?" the president asked.

"I don't know what to do about it."

"General," the president said, loudly. "I am not sure what the public would think or say about the war dead walking the streets of Seattle."

"I understand, sir."

"I asked a Captain Jacobs to get me some reports on similar circumstances, General, reports in which dead soldiers were showing up to loved ones just before DOD notification. Where are those reports?"

"I have them in front of me, Mr. President. I will have them sent over now."

"General, we need this quieted."

I understand, Mr. President."

The president played the news report a seventh time.

THIRTY-FIVE

Maureen O'Grady and Vincent Russo met in the cafeteria of the DOD building before their meeting with Jacobs. That sat in the far back corner of the room, hoping they would not be disturbed or overheard.

"That Seattle report was freaky," Russo said. "Made the hair stand on the back of my neck." Maureen did not respond. "So, both the Farmer and Fisher families told you Jenny and Kimberly were at their homes and in Seattle?"

"Yes. Bill Farmer strictly spoke to me off the record. He doesn't want anything we talked about written down in any report," Maureen said.

"I contacted Cindy Johnson again this morning," Russo said. "She's backing off what she told me yesterday."

"Backing off? She's saying Roy wasn't in Seattle?"

"She's not saying anything."

"She said she saw the Seattle report?" Maureen asked.

"She did."

"She won't say that Roy was there?"

"She won't say yes and she won't say no."

"What do you think?"

"Her no is a good as a yes," Russo commented.

They got up without finishing their coffee and walked directly to the elevator. "Who's going to do the talking?" Maureen asked.

"It doesn't matter. But you have more to report," Russo said.

She nodded as the doors opened.

"Come in," Jacobs said in response to their knock. They both walked in and saluted. "Not necessary," said he told them. "Sit down."

"So, what's up?" Jacobs asked after they were seated.

Maureen looked at Russo then recounted her notification of the Farmers and how Bill Farmer had claimed that Jenny was there right before Maureen delivered the news.

"Isn't this in your report, Lieutenant? Why are you repeating it?"

"I'm not finished, Captain."

She told him what she and Russo had seen when they went to deliver the notification to Harold and Helen Fisher.

"Is it in your report, Lieutenant?" Jacobs was sounding bored.

"Yes, sir."

Before Jacobs could say anything further, she continued, ""Last night when I got home, I received a call from Harold Fisher telling me that Kimberly and five other soldiers had been standing in front of their home. He also confirmed that Kimberly was among the six soldiers in Seattle.

"So the family confirmed one of the soldiers in Seattle was KIA?" Jacobs asked.

"Yes, sir."

"Why are you here, Russo?"

"I was with Lieutenant O'Grady last night, sir."

"Go on."

"I called Cindy Johnson after I saw the Seattle report and asked if she saw the reports and recognized any of the soldiers."

"Why?"

"The Seattle news report mentioned Joe Williams. He was killed with Roy Johnson, Cindy Johnson's husband."

"What did she say?"

"She confirmed that Johnson was in front of her house and in Seattle, apparently simultaneously. She also said she was pretty sure Williams was in both places, too. At least, according to his brother."

"Anything else, Lieutenant?"

"Yes, sir. I made another call to Mrs. Johnson this morning and now she's not saying anything about Seattle."

"She's denying it?"

"She's not saying anything one way or another."

"Your impression?"

"She saw her husband."

"Thank you, both. That is all."

THIRTY-SIX

Cindy Johnson dialed Dave Williams' phone number. She really didn't know how to say what she wanted to say. He answered, friendly but businesslike, at the bar, explaining how crazy things were.

"I can imagine," she said.

"You saw the news report?"

"Yes," she answered.

"It was only on the local channel once," Dave said. "And only once. They never mentioned it again."

"Have they come back to talk with you?"

"No. I have a friend who's a cop, and he's hanging out here as much as he can, running interference."

"That's good, I guess."

"I've also noticed a lot more military vehicles on the street than normal."

"What does that mean?"

"Nothing—maybe."

"Has anyone from the military tried to contact you?"

"Other than the one follow-up call from one of the men who notified us, we haven't had any contact." He thought for a second. "Maybe these extra military vehicles are trying to show that a military presence on the streets of Seattle is not unusual."

"Are the people in the vehicles in full dress uniform?"

"None that I've seen."

"I haven't heard from Sergeant Gordon recently," Cindy said. "I wonder what's going on there, especially after that news report."

"You think the military or the government would try to cover this up?"

"Something's stopped that report. One channel, one run?"

"But why?"

"I don't know, but I don't think like they do." There was a pause. "I've got another call. I'll call you soon." She switched to the incoming call.

"Mrs. Johnson? This is Sergeant Gabriel Gordon."

Her stomach fluttered. A voice, finally, to go along with the writing.

Her thoughts went to her husband trying so hard to save the life of the man on the other end of the phone. For the first time, she questioned his actions. *Why did Roy do it? Duty or respect for life? Something he'd do for anyone? Or was Gabriel Gordon someone he cared about deeply?*

"Sergeant? This is a surprise," her voice cracked.

"For me, too, Mrs. Johnson." It was obvious Gabriel did not know what to say.

"We've been writing so consistently and now a call?" She sat at the kitchen table.

Gabriel explained his confrontation with Chaplain Kirkland and the ongoing interaction with Nancy Savard.

"So," Cindy said, "you and this nurse suspect something?"

"At this point, there's a lot of interest in what's going on. And it seems so odd that the report from Seattle was cut off." He explained what happened in the rec room that day. "And we have not seen it since—the report *or* the channel."

"It was only shown here once," she told him.

"What? It hasn't been rebroadcast in the States?"

"Not even in Seattle." Cindy explained her conversation with Dave Williams.

"What is going on?" Gabriel wondered out loud.

"We're all asking the same question."

Gabriel told her he was trying to get as much information as he could and was working with Nurse Savard. Cindy explained that the last call she had was from one of the soldiers who delivered the KIA notification and that she'd told him was that the last contact she had was in the hangar with Kirkland and Donner.

"Do you think he believed you?"

"No, but they seem to be asking you more questions now." she noted.

"Yes, and they're separating us to ask questions. Oh, and there's a new man in the ward; he was with one of the women when she was killed."

Gabriel told her what he knew about Greg Adams and the rocket attack that killed Kimberly Fisher.

"Are they isolating you men?"

"No, we can move about freely and even visit the other wards. But most of the time, we're together in this ward. We're really the most severely wounded of anyone here."

There was a long pause.

"Mrs. Johnson," Gabriel said, "I need you to gather as much information as you can on this type of thing, especially military. Check other reports from this war, past wars and even police actions."

"How about information from wars the U.S. was not involved in?"

"I hadn't thought about that," he said. "Maybe the U.S. isn't the only country being haunted."

"Haunted?"

"I'm sorry, Mrs. Johnson. I could have said that easier. I loved your husband and Joe Williams; they took care of me like family." Gabriel let the emotion flow into each word. He heard her inhalation coming in short breaths, realizing she could not answer him. Gabriel told her he would call again but would continue to write so as to not draw suspicion, even though he was sure his letters would be intercepted. They hung up.

Cindy went over to her computer and started some Internet searches, entered a number of different search criteria and stopped. She picked up the phone and dialed Dave Williams, Jane Craft and John McCafferty. She explained the call from Gabriel Gordon and asked them all to do similar searches. The more of them researching, the better.

THIRTY-SEVEN

General Fielding Lent met with Commander William Rogers in a large meeting room next to the general's office; just the two of them at the long table. The general was rereading the reports.

"This is the latest?" Lent asked.

"From what I have been told, there is confirmation from each of the families that the KIAs appeared outside that tavern in Seattle."

"Confirmation from anyplace else?"

"There is a hospital ward in Germany where four soldiers, each of whom was wounded at the same time those soldiers died, are being treated. They also recognized the men in Seattle."

"They are all together in one ward?"

"Yes."

"Not sure that's such a good idea," Lent said. "Go on."

"One of the channels that's piped into the hospital showed the report from Seattle."

"They saw it?"

"Most of it. From what I've been able to find out, the entire report did not play. But it was enough for them to recognize the KIAs."

"Jesus," Lent moaned. "So we have confirmation from the families and also men who served with them that the war dead are walking the streets of Seattle."

Commander Rogers got up from the table and went to the door where he signaled Captain Ralph Jacobs to join them. Lent asked him if knew the subject of the meeting. Jacobs nodded.

"How widespread are these sightings of dead soldiers, Captain?" Lent asked.

"The reports you're holding are the only ones I'm aware of."

"Have you done any investigation into other possible sightings?"

"Some, sir, but I've been tied up with these, so my time has been limited. I haven't anyone else to help because I'm not sure how much the information should be spread. If I do the investigation myself, containing it is easier."

Lent agreed with Jacobs' reasoning. He wanted to get as much information as possible without alerting anyone to what the Army and the Department of Defense were doing. After more than fifty years, the government was still handling the Roswell situation. This was more personal and, if word got out, it could go on for centuries.

"Captain," Rogers spoke up." What will you be looking for?"

"Excuse me, sir?"

"In this investigation, what in the reports will alert you to see if further investigation is necessary?"

"What I've done so far is look for blank comments sections or parts of the section that seem missing."

"Are these reports often handed in blank?" Lent asked.

"It's not uncommon. What I'm doing is contacting the notifying officers based on, well, I guess you'd call it a hunch, a feeling I get from reading their reports," Jacobs confessed.

"Can you give us an example?"

"Well, if a man who usually fills out the comments section all of a sudden leaves it blank or with less information than usual, I contact that officer," Jacobs explained. "But even that doesn't get me much, because I can't tell them what I'm looking for from them."

"I want to know more in forty-eight hours, Captain," Lent said. "Is that clear?"

"Yes, sir." Jacobs got up and walked out of the room.

"General, what do you expect to gain by digging into the records?" Rogers asked.

"Hell, I don't know, Bill." Lent spread his arms "The goddamned president wants to know what is going on."

"Will you tell him what you find?"

"I will answer every question I am asked," Lent said. "What else do you know about these men in Germany?"

THIRTY-EIGHT

As Nancy Savard changed Greg Adams' bandages, she reflected that his attitude toward his situation was far different than she would have expected. To have been in a support position—far away from the fighting—and sustain such a life-altering injury was more than a shock, but he seemed to be adjusting well; a natural attitude not Semper Fi. Perhaps he was one of those rare individuals who were able to accept whatever life dealt him and find some positive, no matter how obscure.

"Corporal? How are you doing?" She touched him on the top of his head.

"I guess I'm doing okay, ma'am."

"You guess?"

"Well," he said, his voice rising a bit. "Is there a certain way I should be handling the loss of my legs?"

"It would be understandable if you were upset."

"I am." He looked away. "But what does that do? I can't grow new ones."

Nancy told him that, in addition to being a nurse, she was also a psychiatrist. He looked at her and nodded.

"You want to talk now?"

He nodded again.

She pushed him past the nurse's station and through the doors to the corridor that led to her office. Greg looked at the two soldiers at the far end of the corridor.

"Who are they?" he asked, gesturing.

"I don't know. They're always there, day and night, walking back and forth in front of my office."

"They look like the guys who stand next to Hewson's bed all night."

"Who's the woman who stands near your bed?" Nancy decided to be direct.

Greg said that he had not seen anyone near his bed and didn't realize there was someone other than the soldiers standing at the other beds. Nancy gave him a description.

"Sounds like Kim," he said.

"Kim?"

"Kimberly Fisher. She was killed in the same rocket attack that took my legs," he explained.

"But you haven't seen her at your bed?"

"Nope, but she was outside that Seattle bar," he said.

"The report on the TV? That bar?" she asked.

He nodded.

"What do you think of that report?"

"What is there to think about? You saw the report, and we discussed this last time when Gordon went off on the chaplain. I think it's to be expected."

"That's all? This is normal?"

"It is. I guess you can say those soldiers are still doing their duty."

"Duty?" she said, his answer taking her by surprise.

"Sure, telling loved ones they're okay. And that there's more to things than stupid wars."

"So, having deceased soldiers in wards or the streets of a major city is not unusual to you?"

"No, ma'am—er—doc—what do I call you?"

"Nancy's fine."

"Okay, Nancy. I believe we get all sorts of messages—information, signs—all day long, if we're open to them. This situation is just more obvious than some, like we're being beat over the head with this one," he explained.

"That there are more to things than this silly war?" she asked.

"I think it *is* deeper than just this war. I think it has to do with a message on war in general."

"What is that?"

"That war doesn't work, doesn't solve the problem—any problem. It's time to move on. You'd think, after ten thousand years of slaughtering each other, someone would have come to that realization without the war dead having to point it out to us."

"That's quite a theory," she smiled.

"Nancy," Greg leaned forward, "Have you heard stories before where loved ones reached back as they step across? The most obvious reason is to tell us, their families, and sometimes friends, they're fine. But these soldiers are reaching past family and friends. The message is deeper and more important this time; it's for *everyone*. Why would Kim be showing up in Seattle, where she doesn't know anyone? There *has* to be a deeper message."

Nancy thought for a moment. Soldiers who hadn't served together were showing up at the homes of other soldiers, as if called to do so. They were there for a reason. She had felt it all along. Could Greg be right? Could their message simply be that war needed to end?

"Thank you, Greg," she said. "You've given me something to think about. Let me get you back to the ward." As they were leaving her office she noticed the soldiers were not in their accustomed place in the corridor.

When they were in front of his bed and the wheelchair was positioned. Greg reached for the handle on the overhead frame and lifted himself back on the mattress, nodding to Nancy that he was okay.

"Thank you again, Corporal." She touched him on the hand and wheeled the chair away.

Before she left the ward, she glanced at Gabriel Gordon. He held the cell phone at his side waved it slightly. She nodded and left the ward and walked back to her office. Again, she did not see the soldiers. It felt odd not seeing them. Once inside the office, she noticed the message light blinking on her phone. Looking up in response to a light rap on the door, she could see Lance Kirkland looking in the window. She frowned, but indicated it was okay for him to come in.

"Nancy, how are you today?"

"I'm fine, Captain. What can I do for you?" she said coldly.

"I was wrong with Sergeant Gordon, Nancy," he admitted.

"Yes, Captain, you were."

"Well, can't we straighten it out here?"

"No, Captain. My report will note your demeanor and handling of a seriously wounded soldier."

"For what purpose?" Lance demanded.

"To keep you away from the hospital wards. Maybe they'll send you back to boot camp to deal with recruits trying to get out of the service before their military career even starts."

"It does not have to go that far."

"It does, Captain. Is there anything else?"

As he shut the door behind him, Nancy again realized how odd it was not to see the soldiers walking back and forth.

THIRTY-NINE

Nancy picked up the phone and hit the button to hear the message. It was from Commander William Rogers with the DOD. He mentioned to call him Bill and she wondered if it was because of the obvious connection to Will Rogers. He explained his reason for calling: that he had heard that there were members of one ward sharing some unusual ghost stories.

What is Kirkland's commander's name? Donner! She hung up the phone, staring at the number she'd written down during Roger's brief message.

"Why would the commander of the DOD notification staff be making a call to me?" she thought out loud. Surely he must know of Cindy Johnson and the connection to Lance Kirkland. She dialed the number.

"Lieutenant Commander Nancy Savard for Commander Rogers," she announced.

"Rogers." The commander responded so quickly that she did not even hear the phone connect.

"Good day, Commander," she said. "Nancy Savard returning your call."

"Thank you for the quick return, Lieutenant Commander," Rogers said.

"It's not every day I get a call from the DOD. I figured it was important," she said. "What can I help you with, Commander?"

"It is my understanding that you are personally talking care of three soldiers who have some unusual stories." Rogers continued with what he knew of the soldiers and their experiences.

"It is now four soldiers, Commander. I have just added Greg Adams to the ward. His experiences are similar."

"Experiences? You consider these stories real?"

"They are to these men," she said, deciding to verbally spar until she found out exactly what he was looking for.

"Well, what do you think—uh, what should I call you, doctor or nurse?"

"When we're talking like this, I prefer Nancy. And, yes, I think there is something to the stories, Commander, especially with the Seattle news report."

"What could be the something to the stories?" Rogers asked.

Her detailed response put all the pieces together for him.

"I've never had it all put in one explanation," Rogers admitted. "What is Captain Kirkland's role there?"

So *that's* why you called, Nancy thought. "The chaplain and I have known each other for years. He witnessed one of the dead in a hangar in Arizona."

"What does he think is going on?"

"He denies what he has seen. He should be more open, considering his experiences," Nancy said.

"The Seattle report was seen by these men?"

"Yes, sir."

"What was their reaction?"

"They mostly took it in stride, even though they recognized all of the men and women outside that bar."

"They confirmed the IDs?" Rogers asked.

Nancy verified that they had.

"Nancy," Rogers continued, "You've talked to the men who have gone through physical and mental trauma, but have you considered contacting the families of the men and women who died?"

Nancy expressed her feeling that she had no cause to do so, nor did she have any way to explain her call without possibly causing more stress and emotional upheaval.

"If it is a matter of authorization, I can make a call to your CO if that would help."

"What is the interest in these ghost stories?" she asked.

Rogers was caught off guard by the question but stated that it was far more widespread in the States and had started even before seeing the Seattle news report. "The interest, as you call it, reaches to the highest levels of the U.S. government. So my job is to gather as much information as possible for that highest level of government."

"Thank you, Commander, for the openness."

"So, do you need to run this by your CO or have me call?"

"No, sir. I can make the contact and let him know."

"What do you think Captain Kirkland is doing there, honestly?"

"At first I thought—and still do—that he's gathering information for his CO, and I doubted the interest went above that, at least until now. Captain Kirkland does not have a good way with the men, so he relied on me to get the info."

"You think he knows of the DOD interest?"

"He does if his CO does, and his CO does if you do, sir."

FORTY

The biggest problem Cindy Johnson was having while searching the web was finding the most accurate search criteria. She tried "ghosts" and it brought up too much information and nothing to the specific issue she was searching for. She searched "ghost stories from war" and the results were gruesome pictures of shadowy figures walking across misty fields of broken trees and large holes. The images did make her think these pictures and stories were some of the earliest attempts of the war dead trying to give a message.

Narrowing the search to "war dead appearing to loved ones" brought up basic stories of people who felt a presence or saw a shadow in the house just before getting the news of the death, and the news did not necessarily have to be delivered by the government. But this search brought something different: a picture of a Vietnamese family holding a man who was said to have been killed in battle. The man was never seen again after that picture. In the article, the photographer stated that he did not see the man before or after the picture. The only proof the man had been there was the picture.

She then searched for more information on the Seattle news story, hoping to get links to other sites from there. She was amazed at how the picture had changed. She saw the six soldiers but their faces were no longer easily recognizable. The whole picture seemed grainier. Only by remembering what position he was standing in could she recognize Roy. She bookmarked all the sites.

One of the Seattle sites linked to an Arab site. Even though she couldn't understand the words, the pictures showed emotional families standing next to bodies in pickup trucks. Judging by the wounds on the bodies, the men could have been killed in some kind of battle. What was not obvious was what war or battle took the lives of the men.

She decided to search German war sites. "German war ghosts" brought up many Web pages of pictures of the death camps. Some pictures showed people in civilian dress and in front of these there were women and children wearing prison uniforms, staring at blankly into the camera. The position of the people in prison uniforms and the position of the people in civilian dress were eerily similar to the positioning of the soldiers in the Seattle picture and the bystanders.

She extended the search to include the Korean War, World War I and II, the Spanish-American War and the Civil War. These older wars reflected images of wispy figures on scarred battlefields. Then, progressively, the more recent wars showed pictures of the war dead making contact with loved ones.

Many pictures of the Vietnam memorial showed men in full dress uniform, standing at parade rest looking at the monument. The thing that struck Cindy the oddest was that at least one person in each picture was walking in and out of the lines of soldiers as if they were not aware the soldiers were even there.

"Seems the message has been there all along, but now it's being delivered in a different way. They *are* trying to tell us something," Cindy said out loud. The phone rang and she answered it before the first ring ended.

"Mrs. Johnson?"

"Yes?"

"This is Nurse Nancy Savard."

"Yes?" Cindy was cautious, remembering her conversation with Lt. Russo.

Nancy explained who she was, and then said, "You do know Sergeant Gordon?"

"Yes. How can I help you?" Cindy said.

Nancy explained to Cindy what she had learned from talking to Gabriel Gordon.

""I'm confused." Cindy stopped her. "Aren't you a nurse helping him recover physically? Why would you be involving yourself in his psychological issues?"

"I'm a psychiatrist, Mrs. Johnson. I have a doctorate in psychology. I got my nursing degree so I could help these men on two levels when I treat them."

"I've never heard of that."

"Mrs. Johnson, Gabriel told me he 'saw' your husband with you and your daughter just before the DOD broke the news to you."

"Yes ma'am. He told me the same thing."

"He also told me that he 'saw' Joe Williams visit his brother's bar just before the DOD broke the news to their mother."

"Yes, he mentioned that." Cindy was being very careful.

Nancy recognized her reluctance. "Did you know that Roy and Joe stayed with Gabriel's parents until the word was given to them that Gabriel was out of danger in recovering from his leg wounds?" Nancy said.

"No, he never told me that," Cindy replied. "Nurse, it sounds like you believe these stories."

"I do, Mrs. Johnson. There is something going on," Nancy said, thinking of her discussion with Greg Adams.

"Mrs. Johnson, did Chaplain Kirkland and Commander Donner witness Roy in the hangar?"

"Yes, ma'am. They were there and they saw Roy."

"What did they tell you?"

"The commander has really said nothing. He called me and asked me my impressions, saying that he doesn't know what he saw. But the chaplain really downplayed the whole experience, which is surprising because he had been so supportive up until then. Do you know either of them?"

"I've known the chaplain for over ten years."

"I've been writing to Sergeant Gordon and recently spoke with him by phone," Cindy admitted

"I am aware of these things, Mrs. Johnson." Nancy thought for a moment and then added, "I gave him the cell phone he used to call you."

"Well, it definitely helped to hear his voice," Cindy said, and Nancy thought she was starting to sound more relaxed. "I just recently started to do some searches on the Internet for similar experiences."

"What did you find?"

Cindy explained the images she saw on the Internet from the wars of one hundred to one hundred and fifty years ago, telling Nancy how most of them were just ghostly images of battlefields, but that there seemed to be a growing trend of personal stories and more contact with loved ones as the wars moved forward in time.

"Did you see the Seattle report?" Nancy asked.

"Yes. Roy was there." Cindy told her how the family members recognized Williams, Craft, McCafferty and Farmer.

"We have a new man in the ward who recognized Kimberly Fisher, the second women in the group."

"What is going on? I looked on the Internet and saw the picture from Seattle. I would not be able to recognize Roy now. I only knew it was him from his position in the group."

"What do *you* think is going on, Mrs. Johnson?"

"I think they're trying to give us a message, tell us something. Pictures of wounded, bleeding ghosts and haunted battlefields weren't enough. Their message is being delivered more directly now."

"And what message would that be?"

"Try something different. War is not fixing anything."

"Thank you, Mrs. Johnson. May I call you again?"

"Please do. And, may I ask you, what do you think is going on?"

"I cannot disagree with your assessment," Nancy responded.

"Can you agree? Cindy asked.

"Not yet."

FORTY-ONE

The president read the five reports that were in front of him, paging through each of them more than once.

"These are all pretty much the same story," he said.

"Only the names are different, sir," his aide noted.

"All of these men and women were in front of that Seattle bar?"

"That has been confirmed by two sources, sir: the families and the men who served with them when they were killed."

"What is going on?" the president asked out loud, tossing the reports back on his desk. "I have a picture of my great grandfather walking the Gettysburg battlefield with misty figures standing all around him. I understood he recognized the figures in the picture as men who served with him and who were killed in that battle. But these ghost stories are around every death, not just war deaths. What is going on?"

"Sir," the aide interrupted the president, "there are other reports."

"More KIA appearing?"

"It seems the Seattle report opened up a flood of reports."

"How many?"

"Thousands."

FORTY-TWO

Cindy Johnson resumed her Internet search, entering "Seattle report". That brought up a long list of Web sites, some stating they had the original pictures. Cindy checked the first site and saw the difference. She was right. In the new photos, something had been changed. The one the Web site claimed as the original showed Roy clearly. The Seattle TV station had no explanation about the differences. Actually, they did not respond to any questions about the pictures, to which the Web site said it sounded like a cover-up.

She searched the list of Web site links and found a few that were dedicated to "ghost stories." One site had a forum and a discussion that was even titled "Ghost Stories." While reading the entries in the forum, she became aware of a trend: many of the posters were sharing similar experiences in which the war dead appeared. The stories were not only similar but identical to Roy and Joe's, as well as Steve and Clifford's. She read some stories that were based on second and even third hand reports from the Civil War, Spanish American War and WWI, citing generations that had kept these stories alive. She copied the stories off on a separate sheet, keeping track of the names and e-mail addresses, dates and times.

Is this the only connection? Some forum posted on the internet? Has anyone investigated this fully? Is there a message the dead are trying to get to us?

***

Dave Williams was cleaning up the bar. It was early evening, just before dinner, when Patrolman Kenny McGuire walked in.

"Evening, Dave."

"What's up, Kenny? You change your patrol? You've been here quite a bit."

"Hanging out in the old neighborhood is great," Kenny responded.

"But you still haven's answered my question. Is this your new patrol now?"

"Yeah, Dave," Kenny admitted. "After seeing Joe standing outside the bar, my bosses asked me to change since I know you and the people here."

"Well, it's good to have a familiar face," Dave said.

"Anything new?"

"If you mean have I seen Joe lately, no."

"Well, that and I've also been asked to check if you've had any contacts or questions since Joe was here."

No," Dave said. "I've talked with the wife of the soldier was killed with Joe, but no one else has contacted me."

"What do you two talk about?"

"Mostly just these experiences. Seems she's seen her husband standing in front of her place when Joe is here."

"Does she have any of the others?" Kenny asked as he took off his tie and   gun.
"Off duty?" Dave asked, as he put the gun behind the bar. "Yes," Dave answered Kenny's question. "This last time she had the other five there. They all seemed to match the ones who were here."

Kenny sat down and ordered a club soda.

"Club soda?"

"Yes, for a while. Not sure I feel like drinking tonight. Hey, turn that up." The TV was on but not the sound. It was a picture of some men standing in full dress uniform. It looked like a city in the Orient. Dave picked up the remote.

"…no one knows for sure who these men are, but their uniforms are dress uniforms from 30 years ago. That would be Viet Cong uniforms, ladies and gentlemen." The camera panned the people standing around, many of them crying.

"How many men are standing there?" Kenny asked.

"Looks like twenty to twenty-five."

"…these people have been here for hours…" The TV switched to an interview of a middle-aged man. They were speaking Vietnamese, with the translation showing in the box at the bottom of the screen.

"We heard of these men here earlier today and thought it was just a political demonstration for the old ways. But then someone said that they recognized two of the men in uniform as ones who fought in the war … died in the war."

"Do you recognize any of them?" the interviewer asked.

"I was very young at the time of the war and barely remember him, but this man," he pointed to the man nearest him, "this man looks like my father, from the pictures I have seen of him. He died in the days just before the end of the war."

"Died? Are you saying this man here is dead?"

"He looks like my father and my father died in the war." The man had his arm around an old woman who was weeping and calling to the man in question.

"My mother," the man said holding the woman, "she is sure it is my father." The camera panned the crowd again. Thousands of people filled the area, most of them crying or calling to the soldiers standing in lines.

What the hell is going on?" Kenny asked.

"I don't know," Dave said. "But this ain't right. If those men are dead, why come back after all this time. And if they're alive, what's the purpose?"

"If they *are* dead, what's the purpose? Give me that beer now."

FORTY-THREE

"Hello?" Maureen O'Grady answered her phone. It was Vinnie Russo.

"Your TV on?" he asked. "If not, turn it on."

"What's happening?" Maureen said, clicking the remote. The TV showed a group of men standing in formation. "What is this? Why would we care about some people standing—?" She stopped when she read the scrolling lines at the bottom of the screen. "These guys are dead?"

"They just finished an interview with some guy who said his father was in the group. His father died at the end of the Vietnam War."

"How can he be sure it's his father?"

"Besides what he recognized from pictures, his mother was with him and she recognized the same man as her husband—who was killed at the end of the war."

"What is going on?" Maureen whispered the question again, leaning toward the TV screen.

"Beats the hell out of me," Russo said.

"Is this happening anyplace else?"

"Seattle."

Seattle was different," she responded. "They were appearing to families."

"There are families here."

The TV screen showed an interview with a group of people. The interpretation again scrolled along the bottom of the screen.

We have seen some of these men over the years. Some even came to their families just before the families were notified they were killed in battle. Some never knew any of these men until today.

The TV image moved to another group of men standing on the other side of the same square. The difference was obvious: These were American soldiers wearing dress uniforms from thirty years before. The camera was right up to them, with a reporter asking a question in choppy English.

"Who are you?" the reporter repeated over and over again. The questions were not answered, just met with a slight smile.

Modern military equipment and soldiers moved into the square, carefully setting up a perimeter around both groups of soldiers. When the perimeters were completed, the Americans came to attention, did an about face and started walking in the direction of the Viet Cong soldiers standing on the other side of the square. The men standing at the perimeter took positions to block the marching soldiers; guns were brought to ready. The Americans kept walking. On order, the armed soldiers stood straight up, brought the guns to their side and stood shoulder to shoulder, blocking the advancing Americans.

As the Americans came to within a few steps of the Vietnamese army trying to block their advance, they disappeared—only to reappear on the other side, behind the Vietnamese soldiers. The Viet Cong standing on the other side of the square, each moved to create spaces for the Americans to fill in. Two former enemies were standing together in one formation. The only obvious difference was their uniforms. The Vietnamese army moved quickly to set up new perimeters around the two former forty-year-old enemies.

The TV cameraman backed up, showing a wide angle view of the one group of men, standing quietly at parade rest, almost shoulder to shoulder, looking straight ahead. There was no sound, no reporter's voice, nothing but two dead armies standing together.

"Jesus Christ, Mo, are you seeing that?" Russo's voice added to the chills that Maureen felt running up her back

"Yes," she whispered. "What does it mean?"

FORTY-FOUR

"What is going on?" the president said, looking at the TV.

"I am not sure, sir. I've made a call to the DOD. They confirmed that some of the American soldiers we're seeing have been MIA since the Vietnam War."

The president stared at his aide. "Are you saying that we have government confirmation that these men are dead?"

"What the DOD is confirming, sir, is that these men are missing in action, not dead." The phone rang and the aide picked it up, said nothing and put it down.

"What is it?" the president asked, looking at the aide, whose color was draining from his face.

"That was the DOD. They just confirmed that at least one of the soldiers was KIA. They are looking into the others."

"What is going on?" the president asked.

***

The TV screen switched to Firdos Square in Iraq showing a file film of the statue of Saddam Hussein being pulled down before shifting to the present scene of American soldiers standing in columns.

"We estimate that there are at least four thousand men standing here," the commentator said.

Cindy Johnson stared at the TV screen, trying to recognize the faces of the men standing in full dress uniform and in perfectly straight rows and columns.

"Roy," she whispered in recognition as the face of her husband came on the screen. The camera moved on down the lines of the men.

***

"Joe," Kenny McGuire whispered. Dave nodded.

"Why?" Dave said, breaking down at the sight of his brother.

***

Bill Farmer said, "That's Jenny standing there."

***

"Kimmie." Harold Fisher said.

***

Jane Craft stood at her front door, watching as a soldier in full dress uniform walked up her driveway and stopped at the bottom of the steps. She moved awkwardly, reaching unsteadily for the doorknob and opened the door, stepping outside. Taking a few steps to the right and reaching for the handrail, she lowered herself slowly to sit on the top step. The soldier walked up three steps and sat next to her. This time there was no question about why he was there. Her expression showed the pain and love she was feeling as she slowly lowered her head onto her son's shoulder.

***

Nancy Savard hung up the phone summoning her to the rec room and left her office quickly. When she arrived, the room was packed and she had to push her way toward the front. Her eyes went to the TV screen and she froze at the sight of a formation of American soldiers standing in an Iraqi square. She moved over to Hewson and Gordon, who were in front of the room.

"I've seen Johnson," Gordon said.

"Roy Johnson?" Nancy asked.

"And Joe Williams," Gordon responded, not hiding the tears in his eyes.

"There's Steve McCafferty," Hewson said. "I haven't seen Craft yet."

Allan was in a portable bed next to them. "Jenny Farmer." Allan pointed to a pretty, freckle-faced soldier as the camera panned the lines and lines of American soldiers.

Nancy observed all the other men in the room. All of them were whispering the names of men and women they recognized. The whispers were of disbelief. "But I saw him die."

Greg Adams got Nancy's attention and nodded. She knew that meant he saw Kimberly Fisher. She sat near Gordon and Hewson, with Allan and Adams nearby, joining in their amazement, joy and sorrow, letting her own tears flow down her cheeks. There were stories, happy stories, being told. Nancy laughed with them at their memories. There were also recollections of the horror of how these soldiers died, and she wept as hard as the ones left behind did.

Lance Kirkland walked into the room and Nancy went to him. His eyes were on the TV.

"These are American casualties," he said.

She pointed around the room and then to herself. "Include us."

***

On the TV screen, the Americans shifted to allow a space between the rows and columns. One by one, men wearing traditional Arab clothes took positions in the American formation, standing erectly. It was quickly realized that the end result would be an American standing next to an Iraqi.

A voice on the TV reported similar occurrences in other parts of the world. The picture moved to Richmond, Virginia, where thousands of men in blue and grey dress uniform lined Broad Street. The next image came from Spotsylvania County, Virginia: the Courthouse Battlefield. Then the view shifted to Gettysburg, Pennsylvania, and then to Antietam, New York. Civil War uniforms of blue and gray were spread out on the long green fields of these national monuments.

The TV showed a panoramic scene of Laurel, Montana, with its wide open spaces and softly rolling green hills. The camera zoomed in, depicting a serene look at small town America, showing the rows of small homes and businesses and then focusing on a crowd forming in the downtown area, next to a monument. The crowd was not looking at the monument but at the thousands of Native American Indians standing in no particular order—some wearing traditional war paint, others appearing just in the skins of animals, some barefoot, and some standing next to painted horses.

The monument to Chief Joseph and the words "I will fight no more forever" flashed across the screen.

Different battlefields of Europe were shown, with soldiers in World War I and II uniforms standing in formation, soldiers from many nations standing shoulder to shoulder, with people from the Nazi death camps. The only noticeable separation was the military uniforms or, in the case of the death camps, the prison uniforms. There were images of enemy soldiers who fought in Africa on the fields of those WWII battles standing with the armies of that war and war dead of Rwanda and Darfur, all standing side by side and displaying no differences other than the uniforms.

A voice came on the TV, a kind of narrator who served as little more than the background sound to the images of armies standing together all over the world.

"There are reports coming in from all over the world," the voice said, as the images on the TV screen kept changing, "from every battlefield and every known war, from Ancient Greece and the Holy Land to Vietnam, Bosnia, Iraq and Afghanistan of soldiers and warriors, enemies of thousands of years, standing together, not speaking a word, not showing animosity, no movement or destruction. There must be millions of soldiers." The camera shifted again to the death camps in Germany and then to the South Pacific, where battered and bruised civilians stood at attention—not speaking, just staring. Then the TV feed came in from Hiroshima and Nagasaki, women and children with clothes tattered and smoke rising from their bodies, standing quietly.

"There are civilians standing with these soldiers all over the planet. Confirmation is coming in from all governments that these civilians, as well as their military counterparts, died in war. A war, or, in some cases, many, many wars. The message is obvious. We have to find another way to solve our problems; war is not working, never has and never will."

The reporter fought back his emotion, desperately trying to hold on to enough professionalism and time to make one last point, his breath coming in short gulps as he finished his thought.

"We have given enough."

About the Author

Ken is a Vietnam ERA Navy veteran who did not see combat during that war but was close enough to understand the conflicts that still remain and is passionately against any war. He retired from programming in December of 2008 and finally living his lifelong dream of writing. He lives with his wife, Sandy, in Sedona AZ.

ALL THINGS THAT MATTER PRESS ™

FOR MORE INFORMATION ON TITLES AVAILABLE FROM
ALL THINGS THAT MATTER PRESS, GO TO
http://allthingsthatmatterpress.com
or contact us at
allthingsthatmatterpress@gmail.com

www.ingramcontent.com/pod-product-compliance
Lightning Source LLC
Chambersburg PA
CBHW051651260626
47170CB00004B/1452